The M.   oj Useless Efforts

The Museum of Useless Efforts

Cristina Peri Rossi

El museo de los esfuerzos inútiles

Translated by Tobias Hecht

University of Nebraska Press

Lincoln

Library of Congress Cataloging-
in-Publication Data
Peri Rossi, Christina, 1941–
[El museo de los esfuerzos inútiles.
English] The museum of useless
efforts / Cristina Peri Rossi ;
translated by Tobias Hecht. p.
cm. ISBN 0-8032-3726-X (cl :
alk. paper) — ISBN 0-8032-8764-X
(pa : alk. paper) I. Title.
PQ8520.26.E74 M7713 2001
863'.64—dc21   00-059966
Publication of this book was
assisted by a grant from the
Program for Cultural Coopera-
tion between Spain's Ministry of
Culture and Education and
United States' Universities.

Ce sont les vertiges qui sont mes rivières vives.

Henri Michaux, *La vie dans les plis*

The category through which the world manifests
itself is the category of hallucination.

Gottfried Benn, *Double Life*

An authentic short story must be both a prophetic
representation – an ideal representation – and an
indispensable representation. Authentic authors of
short stories are visionaries.

Novalis, *Fragments*

It is the *formation*, not the form, that is mysterious.

Gaston Bachelard

This translation is dedicated to Carlos Narváez

Contents

The Museum of Useless Efforts

Every afternoon, I visit the Museum of Useless Efforts. I ask for the catalog and take a seat at the large wooden table. The book's pages are a little faint, so I like to run through them slowly, as if I were turning the leaves of time. I never see other readers, which is probably why the clerk pays so much attention to me. Since I'm one of the few visitors, she spoils me. She's probably afraid of losing her job, what with the lack of public demand. Before entering, I take a close look at the sign hanging on the glass door. In uppercase letters it reads, 'HOURS: MORNINGS, 9:00–2:00. EVENINGS, 5:00–8:00. CLOSED MONDAYS.' I almost always know which useless effort I want to look up, but sometimes I ask for the catalog so the girl will have something to do.

'Which year would you like?' she'll ask courteously.

'The 1922 catalog,' I might answer.

After a little while she'll return with a thick book bound in deep red leather and place it on the table, in front of my seat. She's very accommodating, and if she thinks there isn't enough light coming through the window, she'll switch on the bronze lamp herself, adjusting its green glass shade so that the light falls across the pages of the book. Sometimes I make a brief comment when I return the catalog. For example, I might tell her, 'Nineteen twenty-two was a very busy year. A lot of people were determined to make useless efforts. How many volumes are there?'

'Fourteen,' she answers in a very professional voice.

So I have a look at some of the useless efforts of that year, children who tried to fly, men bent on amassing riches, complicated mechanisms that never actually worked, and a lot of couples.

'Nineteen seventy-five was a far more bountiful year,' she says with a touch of sadness. 'We still haven't recorded all of the entries.'

'The classifiers must have their work cut out for them,' I think out loud.

'That's right,' she replies. 'They've only just made it to the letter C, and several volumes have already been published. And that's without counting the repeats.'

Curiously, useless efforts get repeated, but the repeats aren't included in the catalog. That would take up too much space. With the aid of various contraptions, a man tried to fly seven times; some prostitutes attempted to find another job; a woman wanted to paint a picture; someone sought to overcome fear; nearly everybody tried to be immortal or lived as if they were.

The clerk assures me that only a tiny proportion of useless efforts makes it to the museum. For one thing, the government lacks money, so acquisitions, exchanges, or exhibits in the provinces or abroad are practically impossible. For another, the inordinate number of useless efforts carried out all the time means that a lot of people would have to be willing to work without pay or understanding on the part of the public. Sometimes, when getting official support seems hopelessly unlikely, appeals are made to the private sector. But the returns have been few and discouraging. Virginia (that's the name of the nice clerk who often talks

2

with me at the museum) explains that all the private sources appealed to proved as demanding as they were unsympathetic, failing to understand what the museum is about.

The building is located on the outskirts of the city, in a vacant lot full of cats and refuse where, just slightly below ground level, you can still find cannonballs from an ancient war, rusty sword handles, and donkey jawbones decayed by time.

'Do you have a cigarette?' Virginia asks me with an expression that fails to mask her anxiety.

I search my pockets, finding an old slightly chipped key, the tip of a broken screwdriver, the return ticket for the bus, a button off my shirt, a few coins, and – finally – two crumpled-up cigarettes. She smokes furtively, hidden amid thick books (whose spines are peeling), the timepiece on the wall that always indicates the wrong hour of day (usually an hour gone by), and the old, dust-covered decorative molding. It is believed that on the spot where the museum now stands there was once, in the days of war, a fortress. Its thick foundation stones were put to some practical use, some timbers as well; the walls were shored up. The museum opened its doors in 1946. Some photographs of the ceremony survive: men wearing tails; ladies in long dark skirts, sequins, and hats with birds or flowers on them. Behind them, you can imagine an orchestra playing ballroom pieces. The guests have an air between solemn and absurd, as if they were slicing a cake decorated with an official ribbon.

I forgot to mention that Virginia has a slight squint. This minor defect gives her face a touch of humor that diminishes its naïveté. As if her wandering gaze were a floating, humorous comment, detached from any context.

The useless efforts are classified by letter. When all the letters have been used, numbers are added. It's a slow, complicated process. Each effort has its own pigeonhole, page, and description. Walking among them with extraordinary agility, Virginia looks like a priestess, the virgin of an ancient but timeless religion.

Some of the useless efforts are beautiful, others somber. We don't always agree about their classification.

Leafing through one of the volumes, I found a man who spent ten years trying to make his dog talk. Another spent more than twenty trying to win a woman's affections. He would bring her flowers, plants, and butterfly catalogs, offer her trips, write poems, compose songs; he built her a house, forgave all her mistakes, and tolerated her lovers. Then he committed suicide.

'It was hard work,' I say to Virginia, 'though possibly stimulating.'

'That's a somber story,' Virginia replies. 'The museum has a detailed description of the woman. She was a frivolous, moody, fickle, lazy, embittered little thing. She was also selfish and somewhat dim-witted.'

There are men who have taken long journeys in pursuit of inexistent places, unrecoverable memories, deceased women, disappeared friends. There are children who undertook impossible tasks with great resolve. Like the ones who would dig a hole periodically washed over by the waves.

In the museum, smoking and singing are forbidden. The prohibition on singing seems to affect Virginia as much as the one on smoking. 'I'd like to hum a little song now and again,' she confides wistfully.

People whose useless effort consisted in attempting to reconstruct their family tree, digging for gold, writing a book. Others who had hoped to win the lottery.

'I prefer the travelers,' Virginia tells me.

4

Entire sections of the museum are dedicated to voyages. We reconstruct them from the pages of the books. After a time of drifting across various seas, traversing dense forests, discovering cities and marketplaces, crossing bridges, sleeping on trains and station benches, the travelers forget the purpose of the trip yet nevertheless continue traveling. And then one day – lost in a flood, trapped in the subway, asleep forever in a doorway – they disappear without a trace. And no one comes to claim them.

Virginia tells me that there used to be private investigators, amateur enthusiasts who supplied the museum with material. I can even recall a time when it was fashionable to collect useless efforts, as one might do with stamps or ant colonies.

'I think the abundance of items destroyed their appeal,' Virginia states. 'It's only exciting to search for scarce things, to find the unusual.'

Back then, people would come to the museum from different places and request information. A certain case would pique their curiosity. They would leave with forms and return bearing stories they had copied down, with the appropriate photographs attached – useless efforts turned over to the museum, like butterflies or rare insects. For example, the story of the man who struggled for five years to prevent a war, until his head was blown off by the first shot fired from a cannon. Or Lewis Carroll, who spent his entire life trying to avoid drafts but died from a cold because one time he forgot his raincoat.

I don't know whether I've mentioned that Virginia has a slight squint. I often enjoy following her gaze, never knowing where it will fall next. When I see her crossing the room, burdened with folders, books, and all sorts of documents, I can't resist the impulse to get up from my seat and lend her a hand.

Sometimes, in the middle of a task, she'll complain a little. 'I'm tired of going back and forth,' she might say. 'We'll never manage to classify everything. And then you have the newspapers. They're full of useless efforts.'

Such as the story about the boxer who tried to recover his title five times. He was finally disqualified when he took a bad blow to the eye. Now he probably wanders around some squalid neighborhood, from one bar to the next, remembering what it was like when his eyesight was good and his punches were lethal. Or the story of the trapeze artist who suffered from vertigo and couldn't look down. Or the one about the dwarf who wanted to grow and traveled all over the place in search of a doctor who could cure him.

When she gets tired of moving books around, she sits on a pile of old, dusty newspapers, lights a cigarette – discreetly, because smoking isn't permitted – and thinks out loud.

'We probably need to hire someone else,' she might say in a tone of resignation. Or, 'I have no idea when they'll pay me this month's salary.'

I've invited her to take a walk in the city, to go out for coffee or to the movies. But she doesn't want to. Only inside the gray, dusty walls of the museum is she willing to talk with me.

If time is elapsing, I wouldn't know, because my afternoons are so busy. But Mondays are days of sadness and abstinence and leave me not knowing what to do, how to live.

The museum closes at eight o'clock in the evening. Virginia turns the simple metal key in the lock; any other measures would be unnecessary because it's unlikely anyone would try to break into the museum. Only once did a man try, Virginia tells me. He wanted his name removed from the catalog. As an adolescent he had made a useless effort that later he felt embarrassed about, and he wanted to eliminate any trace of it.

6

'We caught him in time,' Virginia explains. 'It was very hard to talk him out of it. He kept insisting that his effort was private in nature and that he wanted us to return it to him. That time I put my foot down. It was a rare piece – practically a collector's item. The museum would have suffered a huge loss had the man gotten his way.'

Melancholy, I leave the museum at closing time. In the beginning I found that the time it took for one day to become the next was unbearable. But I've learned to wait. I've also grown accustomed to Virginia's presence, and I can't imagine how the museum would be able to exist without her. I know that the director (the one in the photograph with the two-tone sash across his chest) feels the same way: he's decided to give her a promotion. In the absence of any organizational structure consecrated by law or common practice, he has created a new position, which is actually identical to her previous one, only it has another name. Reminding her of the sacred nature of her mission, he has named her Priestess of the Temple – guardian, at the museum's entrance, of the fleeting memory of the living.

Up on the Rope

From the moment I was born, I've been very fond of the rope. At first it was a tight rope, but over time it grew looser. That didn't matter, because I was well adapted to it. My toes were like hooks and stuck to the rope so I didn't have to worry about falling off. And I never got off the rope: I liked being in the air all the time. I would eat my meals, read, listen to music, make little wicker things – coasters, table mats, and baskets – while walking around up there.

When I was little, my parents hired a nice man to watch over me. He was a retired civil servant who ran from one end of the room to the other with a burlap bag stretched between his hands in case I fell. The poor man had his work cut out for him because, being a restless child, I was always dashing from one end of the rope to the other, and he had to chase after me with the sack wide open. The old man would pant, beads of sweat would gather on his brow, and sometimes he would ask me to stay still so he could rest for a while. I wasn't very talkative, which made his job lonely and tedious. But he can take credit for my knowledge of the arts and sciences. Whenever I would stop somewhere on the rope, he would teach me about the laws of physics or poetic meter. He was a good man and loved me like a son. He would always say he was tired, that he wasn't cut out for the job, that he was too old, that he was only doing it because his pension was too small to live on. So if he was a little remiss in his work, if he stopped running underfoot from one end of the room to another and took a moment to roll a cigarette or have a glass of wine, I wouldn't object.

Sometimes I would play tricks on him. I'd move across the rope as always, taking firm, cautious steps. But when I got to the middle, I would pretend to slip. The poor man would scamper to a spot just below me and open the bag all the way so he could catch me. But I wouldn't fall. In fact, I don't remember ever having fallen. Anyway, I had my doubts about whether he was fit enough to make it in time if I really had. He walked very fast and was attentive (with one eye, he would follow my steps across the rope), but the speed of my fall might have been quicker than his legs.

Playing a trick on him, one day I feigned a scream when I'd almost reached one end of the rope. Terrified, the old man scurried over, and I dropped a pink mouse I'd hidden in my pocket into his open sack. The mouse fell right into the bag, but the old man had closed his eyes and didn't discover it until later. He got very upset with me that time and almost quit. I offered a heartfelt apology and pleaded with him to stay down there; his presence, what he would do with the bag, the stories he would tell me during the odd peaceful moments, his crazy running around were all very stimulating. And in reality, I'd already decided not to get down. I let him know this a few days later. He didn't act surprised or try to dissuade me, and I was grateful for that. He immediately began making arrangements so my life up there wouldn't be uncomfortable. First, he hoisted up a table so I could eat without making a mess of myself. Then, some articles for my personal hygiene. Using an ingenious system of ropes and pulleys, he supplied me with whatever I needed but didn't have at hand: a bar of soap, a newspaper, candles (blackouts are common here), the odd book, scissors, a clean shirt. I was already an adolescent and he was very concerned about my education. He set up a chalkboard on the wall and would work out formulas and discuss the geography of Ireland while I sat on the rope. Later, he got a slide projector that was put to use throughout the remainder of my education.

'If I were younger,' he would tell me, 'I would try to live up there too.'

He believed every creature had its place – the earth, the air, the water – and he saw no reason why mine should not be the rope. He even assured me that only a change in instincts could alter something like that, which is why terrestrial beings suffer on airplanes, aerial beings don't like boats, and seamen get dizzy in cities.

Walking around, I would listen to him with interest. Although I lived in constant danger (any distraction at all – an unanticipated onset of drowsiness, a misstep, a failure of my quick reflexes – could send me plummeting into the abyss), I was also spared other dangers. I would toss banana peels into the garbage – with great accuracy – recite verses from Amado Nervo, and play old Indian melodies on the harmonica; sometimes, from up above, I would oversee the placement of a piece of furniture or fix the electrical wires. Only the prospect of visitors terrified me. I didn't want to see anyone, and I had ordered the old man to throw out any intruders. Whenever someone would unexpectedly enter the room, I would move to one end of the rope, right next to the ceiling, and try to disappear, become a dark insect. I reckoned that from down below, the visitor wouldn't see anything but the cord swaying in space, like a cable over the ocean.

'If I were younger,' the old man would insist, 'I'd get up there with you, to rest.'

10

One day, the man brought his daughter to meet me. He didn't give me any warning, which upset me. I hid behind the chandelier. It was one of those big chandeliers you find in theaters or in the drawing rooms of aristocratic houses, with a lot of decorative prisms. Sometimes, just to keep myself busy, I would polish the prisms with a cloth moistened in vinegar. From my corner, I saw her enter. She was wearing black high-heeled shoes and took cautious steps. She had on a beige raincoat and her hair was short. I didn't think the rope spectacle could possibly interest her. Since my early childhood, I had refused to perform tricks or do exercise on the rope. I would just stroll around, and I despised gymnasts and acrobats who entertained the public at the circus or in shows.

She proceeded to the center of the room and looked up. The floorboards creaked a little. The old man sat down in a chair, like an usher after the performance has begun. I let her look for me, knowing I would be difficult to spot. I thought she would get tired of looking for me because she wasn't used to bending her neck to look up at high things. The old man started reading the paper. It was a way of leaving me alone in the face of danger.

'Oh! What a beautiful picture,' she murmured, as she discovered a Turner reproduction on the wall. I had cut it out and stuck it there. If it hadn't been beyond my reach, I would have yanked it off the wall to prevent her from looking at it. Unfortunately, the room was full of newspaper clippings, photographs, and objects I enjoyed displaying on the shelves. And she seemed bent on taking inventory.

'Don't touch that!' I yelled from my corner as she reached for one of my kaleidoscopes. 'I only allow the old man to touch it – so he can dust it.'

She withdrew her hand and looked toward the corner where I was.

Then she did something completely unexpected. She nimbly climbed up on a chair, to get closer to me. That bothered me. No one had ever dared to do that, not even the old man when I would ask him for something; he always found a way to get things up to me, using the pulley system.

'Get down from there!' I yelled, overcome with rage.

She didn't budge. She was on a wicker chair, which I was hoping would collapse under her weight. Unfortunately, because I had plaited it myself, it was very sturdy.

'I would like to see your face,' she told me, ignoring my order.

I could see hers. It was sort of round and nice, vivacious and carefree. I closed my eyes. I would have preferred her to look like the old man, whose face was weathered by time, anxiety, and uncertainty. When I opened my eyes again, she was still standing on the chair, motionless like a statue.

'I've brought something for you,' she said, trying to get on my good side. I knew that trick. My parents, my neighbors, even a doctor had tried it many times. Little objects meant to discourage or encourage me or persuade me of something.

'I don't need anything,' I said firmly.

I don't know why, but I suspected she had a camera in her clothing and that she was planning to take my picture. People do things like that. But it must have been my imagination: the old man wouldn't have allowed her in with a hidden camera.

All of a sudden, she got down from the chair. She fixed her shoes, straightened her olive-colored skirt, and said to the old man, who was pretending to read, 'It's true, he doesn't need anything.'

'Just like I told you, little one,' the old man mumbled.

Then I emerged, not all the way, just enough so that she could see me. I took a few steps across the rope and looked at her.

She raised her head and smiled. I liked her smile. It was similar to the old man's smile.

'You know?' she said in a quiet, humble, almost confessional voice, 'I'm dying to get up there. It's what I've always wanted.'

I was silent.

'As a matter of fact, I have too,' the old man murmured right away. 'But you know, what with my age, my ailments, the heat, the cold, I can't stay on my feet for long. I'm not even worried about the bag anymore. He doesn't need it. Not the bag, not me. He doesn't need anyone.'

'I've always wanted to go up there,' she repeated, raising her eyes in wonder. She had this imploring expression that disturbed me.

'Maybe, if I were younger,' the old man went on, 'I would try it. But at my age, almost everything except rushing around in an empty room with a bag in my hands is off limits.'

'If you wouldn't mind,' the girl mumbled, 'if you would let me try. . . .'

'That's impossible,' I said gently. 'It's not a matter of selfishness. . . .'

'Just once. Just this once, I promise,' she pleaded. 'It would be like going out on a boat when you're little, or taking a ride on a hot-air balloon, or visiting the island where the pelicans live. It's the dream of a lifetime, just once. . . .'

'I can't,' I answered quietly.

'If you let me, I won't cause any trouble. I just want to get up there for a moment and then come back down. . . .'

'You'd want to stay forever,' I predicted.

'No, I promise, I wouldn't. Just once, for a moment.'

'I also wanted to,' the old man added, 'but the legal considerations, my gout, my age. . . . But I still dream of it.'

'Just once, to try it,' she suggested.

'No, it's impossible,' I tried to persuade her. 'There's no room here. Besides, you'd fall. There's only room for one person. With two of us, we'd hurt each other.'

'I'm not afraid of dying,' she said.

'It just can't be,' I replied. 'It's not up to me. It's a question of physics, of nature. We have to respect those things. But you can get up on a chair and talk with me if you'd like. You can scale a mountain, get on a plane, or ride a cable car. But you can't get up here, it's impossible.'

Saddened, she lowered her eyes.

'I told you,' the old man scolded her. 'That's the way it is.'

'It would have been so wonderful,' she sighed, resting her head on the old man's shoulder.

To make her forget her sadness, I danced a few steps on the rope. It was something that normally I would never do, but I felt sad for her.

She went away. I returned to my activities on the rope: I polished the prisms, made a wicker basket to store handkerchiefs in, played the harmonica, read an old newspaper, pasted a few more clippings on the wall, wrote a poem and a letter.

The next day I woke up to find the old man rushing into the bedroom, looking jittery. He was panting and seemed to be running away from something. I could hear a lot of commotion outside.

'What's going on?' I asked, frightened.

The old man shut the door firmly and leaned against it.

'There's a crowd gathering out there,' he said.

Several explanations occurred to me: a sporting victory, a demonstration, an accident, the appearance of an actress. The crowd was growing larger, and I could hear it getting closer and closer. Nervously, I paced along the rope. The old man was still leaning against the door. I heard shouts, exhortations, whistles, pounding.

'What do they want?' I asked the old man, who had broken into a sweat.

He pointed at the rope. 'They all want to get up there,' he answered, exhausted.

Mona Lisa

The first time I saw Gioconda, I fell in love with her. It was an indistinct, misty autumn. In the distance, the contours of trees and smooth lakes faded away, as sometimes happens in paintings. A light mist that clouded our faces, rendering us vaguely unreal. She was dressed in black (the fabric, however, transparent), and I think someone told me she had lost a child. I saw her in the distance, as happens with apparitions, and from that instant I became extremely sensitive to anything that had to do with her. She lived in another city, as I discovered. Sometimes, to alleviate her sorrow, she took short strolls. Immediately – sometimes quite slowly – I discovered the things she favored. I conjured up her pleasures even without knowing them and, with that rare ability of someone in love to notice small details, I endeavored to surround myself with objects that would please her, like a meticulous collector. For want of her, I became a collector, seeking solace in things related to her. For someone who loves, nothing is superfluous. Giocondo, her husband, was engaged in a dispute with a painter, as I found out. He was a prosperous and crude merchant, enriched by trading in textiles, and like those of his class sought to surround himself with valuable things, though he would chaffer over their price. I quickly discovered the name of the city where they lived. It was a melodious, sweet name; I was sur-

16

prised, because I should have guessed it. A city of water, bridges, and little windows built many centuries ago by merchants, ancestors of Giocondo who, in order to compete with the nobles and bishops, had hired architects and painters to enhance the city's beauty, like a lady might do with chambermaids. He lived in an old refurbished palace, the façade of which he had had inlaid with gold. But my informant drew my attention to the most beautiful thing about the palace's façade: a small landscape, a watercolor protected by a wooden frame, depicting a countryside. At the center of the landscape, a vaporous lake where a barely insinuated skiff rose above the water. 'That, I am certain, must have been commissioned by Gioconda,' I thought to myself.

I must confess that since I laid eyes on her, I have slept little. My nights are full of commotion, as if I had drunk too much or ingested some innervating drug. When I go to bed, my imagination unfurls, febrile and disorderly. I work out ingenious projects, formulate thousands of plans, my ideas buzzing about like drunken bees. The excitement is so acute that I break into a sweat and scurry to begin different tasks, these, in turn, interrupted by others until daybreak when, exhausted, I fall asleep. I awake confused, recalling little of what I had planned during the night. I feel depressed until the image of Gioconda returns some meaning to my days and makes me happy, like a secret possession (I am not a bad draftsman and I confess I have made some sketches of her face, based on my recollection of the first time I saw her).

I have completely neglected my wife – how could I explain to her what has happened without betraying Gioconda? I no longer share her bed and I endeavor to spend all my time away, lost amid the woods tenuously drawn in the autumn mist. The faint woods and the lakes I conjured up the first time I saw Gioconda and that now accompany all my images of her. One falls in love with certain places relentlessly associated with the beloved and strolls among them, alone but intimately accompanied.

I endeavor to obtain information about the city where she lives; I fear some unexpected danger may stalk it. I imagine terrible catastrophes: volcanic eruptions, tidal waves, fires, the insane acts of men – the cities of our times rival one another in aggressiveness and envy. In my mind, I aim to hold back the waters of the rivers that cross her city, and I take the opportunity to stroll with her across bridges – those delightful, intimate, moist wooden bridges that creak under our soles. (I must confess that the first time I saw her, enraptured by the beauty of her face, I did not take notice of her feet. What gaps there are in our power of observation! Nonetheless, it is not impossible to reconstruct them, based on the perfection of other lines. I realize that this harmony is not always humanly possible, but what is surprising about her is precisely the harmonious, serene, incremental development of her features, such that, from a fragment, the whole can be imagined.)

The passage of time does not concern me. Only too well do I know that her beauty, endowed with a certain diaphanous quality, an inner grace that transcends the progression of months, the passing of autumns, will withstand it. Only terrible harm, the intervention of an assassin's hand, could disturb that harmony. And Giocondo does not worry me. Engaged as he is with his financial transactions, indifferent to any type of value that cannot be hoarded in a well-guarded coffer, his relations with her are as superficial as they are harmless. Which, to a certain extent, spares me from jealousy.

For some time now, I have been miserly. I save in every way I can so as to set aside enough money to make the journey I have

18

dreamed of. I have stopped smoking and frequenting the tavern, I do not purchase clothing, and I am extremely vigilant with regard to the upkeep of the house. Whatever small repairs are necessary at home I do myself, and I make use of all those things squandered by dissolute men who are not in love, probably because they no longer dream. I have painstakingly studied the ways to reach that city and am certain that shortly I will be able to set out on the journey. That dream fills my days with intensity. I make no attempt to communicate with Gioconda. I am certain that when I saw her, she did not take notice of me, nor would she have taken notice of any man. She was overcome with sorrow and her eyes looked without seeing, contemplating, if anything at all, things that were of the past, things hidden in the still lakes where I continue to conjure her up. When my wife questions me, I answer in vague terms. It is not a matter of simply keeping my secret: the most heartfelt things almost never withstand translation into words.

But I know, I am certain, I will be able to find her. Somewhere in the city, her unmistakable features await me. As for Giocondo, he seems to still be engaged in a dispute with a painter. He doubtless does not want to pay for a canvas or, if he is owed something, plans to throw the painter out of his atelier. Giocondo has the insolence characteristic of the rich, and the poor painter has to make a living. My informant explains that the feud has gone on for close to three years and that the painter has sworn revenge. What would my Gioconda say about all this? Despite the reputation women in that city have for being nosy, I am certain she is wholly unaware of her husband's affairs. The loss of her child is still recent and she is unable to find solace. Attempting to entertain her, Giocondo hires musicians who sing and dance in the garden, but she seems not to hear them. Gioconda, mournful notwithstanding her décolletage. Regrettably, I am not a musician. If I were, I might have access to your castle. I would play the flute like no one has ever played it before, conjuring up the lakes and woods where you stroll in autumn, lakes seemingly suspended above which a skiff sometimes rises. I would compose verses and sonatas until you gently, almost unwillingly, smile, as if offering a small reward for my efforts. Oh Gioconda, that smile would be a vague acknowledgment, confirmation of your having heard.

I have arrived in the city of bridges, of circular lakes and misty woods that disappear on the horizon amidst placid clouds. I have walked the narrow, winding streets with their fluffy dogs and markets brimming with golden fruit and silken fabrics. Everywhere the peddling: the oranges shine; fish just plucked from the sea; the merchants' offers buzz; avid buyers scrutinize gold vessels, acquiring carefully set, sumptuous jewels, feuding over valuable pieces. The streets are damp, and in the distance a serene forest is outlined.

Forthwith, I sought someone with information about the Giocondo family. It was not difficult: everyone knows them in this city, but for some reason, when I questioned people, they wanted to change the subject. I have offered money, the few coins I have left after the journey, but this is a prosperous city and my fortune small. I tried with traders who courteously offered me cloths and products from India, and then with the gondoliers, who take passengers from one part of the city to another. I should say that one of the most lively pleasures to be enjoyed here is that of traversing certain regions in those delicate, slender crafts (which they adorn in fine taste and treat with the utmost care, as if they were precious objects); they glide beneath the wooden bridges, scarcely

20

stirring the green waters. Finally, a young man, whom I chose for his humble appearance but intelligent gaze, agreed to inform me. He revealed something terrible: the painter that Giocondo had hired and with whom he had been feuding for years decided to seek revenge. He painted a slender mustache on the lips of Gioconda, and no one has been able to remove it.

The Runner Stumbles

He saw the towering trees, the green leaves, a distant nest (or was it simply a mesh of twigs?), the sky's cupola, the clouds speeding around the track like white runners, the clouds rushing toward the finish line, he saw the moon at midday, the moon that had appeared silently, discretely, situating itself at an almost imperceptible angle to the landscape, the birds with their games, their own tournaments, ceaselessly flying here and there, he saw dark wings cutting through the air, sumptuous movements, with his eyes he followed their unforeseeable course, their routes; collapsed, on the ground, through astonished eyes, he saw all that.

He was on the fourteenth lap. He was a good runner. The newspapers had predicted he would win, even set a new record. For years they had been waiting for a new record, people are always waiting for things like that. And now there was that theory suggested by a Brazilian physicist, probably a lunatic, it seemed to him: the speed of light is not always the same. 'What could that mean?' he asked himself. The newspapers had said that he might break the record. So, had Einstein been wrong? Or was it that light was trying to break a record, just like he was? And people were crowding around the track, the fifteenth lap, he was in the lead, way ahead, because he was born to run, the sun radiating heat, so much heat (what did *born to run* mean?), these marvelous feet. The announcer saying, 'An extraordinary pace on the sixteenth lap, two-thirds of the way there,' long-distance runner, steady pace. From the start he hadn't hesitated to break away from the rest of them, to make it clear from the outset who was going to win; if they thought he was going to hold back, reserve his energy and not break off from the pack, save the final struggle – the merciless struggle – for the final few meters, they were wrong: free of their elbows, with no one in his way, with the whole track ahead of him, he was running as fast as light, that is if light travels through space at a constant velocity. Somewhere – outside the oval-shaped track he was running around time and again, torturously, like in a dream – his coach would be nervously checking his watch. So the speed of that ray of light that hit the track was not constant? Constant, like his pace? Lap number nineteen, only seven more to go, for that ray of light hurled like a yearning runner; everyone else was behind him, he'd passed them several laps back, so it was just a matter of beating someone, the legendary runner who'd set the last record, up to now the definitive record, if light moves at a constant speed. On the twenty-first lap, he felt he was about to achieve his goal; although fatigued, his rhythm was excellent, he was progressing around the track at a steady pace, his movements nimble and light, like those of a gazelle – in the words of the announcer – elegant, as if for him there was nothing difficult about running. In a confused sort of way, he could make out the faces of the spectators, but there was no need to see them more clearly, only the track was circulating in his brain, the coach would have his eyes riveted on his stopwatch. Then he lapped the young runner with red hair and blue shorts whose tired pant didn't bode well for him, then runner number seventeen, trailing far behind, several laps back, still on a lap he'd left long ago, with the spot of sun on the track. Everyone's eyes were clouding over, their eyes filling with sweat, throbbing. According to his count, he had only three laps to go, three laps till the little man with the chessboard-like flag would let him collapse after crossing the finish line, the finish line, the end of the track, the ribbon that would say the insane race was behind him, and he heard a shout, just one shout, and it was his coach who must have been announcing that he was about to do it, that he was going to set a new record, clock the best time in the world for the ten thousand meters, ten thousand perfectly flat meters.

That was when he felt an enormous urge to stop. It wasn't that he was so tired; he had done his training and the experts had all said he would win the race; in reality, he had only been running to set a new record. And now this undeniable urge to stop. To fall on the side of the track and never get up again. Careful: if a runner's down, you can't touch him. If he gets up on his own, he can continue running. But not if someone helps him to get back up on his feet. This uncontrollable urge to sit down on the side of the track and look at the sky. Surely, he thought, he'd see the trees. A fistful of branches with quivering leaves, and up at the top, a nest. The smallest leaves fluttering in the wind, in the light wind that alters the speed of light forever, which is no longer constant, according to the Brazilian physicist. 'I'm nothing special, ma'am,' he'd told a slightly senile fan the other night. 'I'm just an expert at organizing time.'

Excited, the coach gave him a signal: just one lap to go. Just one more. And his pace remained steady. He passed a panting runner who had his hand on his waist. Oh, that sharp pain below the ribs, that pressure that makes it hard to breathe. If you feel it, you're done for and you may as well get off the track. But out of self-respect, you can't. That pain was in the spleen, an organ people rarely discuss because it only bothers you when you've exerted yourself in some unusual way, when you've run too much, as he'd learned after years of training. And this strange, uncontrollable desire to quit, to stop on the side of the track, to look at the trees, to breathe deeply. Every lap is the same, in your memory one merges with another and you don't know if you're on the twenty-third or the twenty-fourth, on the sixteenth or the seventeenth. Like that poor guy who thought he'd reached the finish line and threw himself on the ground. Someone – his coach, probably, or one of the referees – came up to him and, without touching him, gave him the news that he wasn't there yet, that he'd miscounted: he still had three laps to go. And there he was, unable to get up off the ground, his muscles stiff. And if he got up, it would only be to continue running – if he didn't faint first, that is.

Nothing like that would ever happen to him. He ran naturally, as if running were the most normal thing in the world, as if he could run forever. Regularly, but with a constant, unchanging velocity, unlike that of light, which had betrayed him, which now seemed to move inconsistently. He was on the verge of breaking a record. And then, the ecstasy of allowing himself to fall; that hallowed, sublime ecstasy of stopping, of softly slipping off the track, just a few meters from the end, just a little before the finish line, of slipping calmly to the ground and raising his head, oh those tall trees, the blue sky, the slow clouds, the curly branch ends, the leaves fluttering, raise his eyes and watch the measured flight of birds, there's gibberish all about but he does not hear it, words of reproach surely, insults surely, his coach exasperated, seeing the other runners pass by, their shorts, some positively panting, that one with his hand on his side, you won't finish, you

25

won't make it, but up above, the trees were floating, floating in an illusory realm no one could see, now the blond runner with a cramp, hobbling on – have I ever seen that bird before? – the announcer telling of the incredible success, like light, his speed is constant, but he had the urge to stop. And he raised his eyes toward the sky.

Tarzan's Roar

Johnny Weissmuller roared and the entire jungle (with its suggestive vines and dense foliage) seemed to tremble. The whisky tumbler slid off the small glass table and fell onto the lion-skin rug, leaving a dark, circular, rain-swollen lake. Johnny roared: a long, enduring roar with its outer crust and littoral, its mountains of sound, its lichen-rimmed caves, its hidden depths where bats fly and nimble clouds waft off like smoke. Protracted, deep; long, profound – a roar that soared through the air from branch to branch, summoning the blue birds and gray elephants, a roar that pierced the chiaroscuro of the leaves and the scarred trunks, that whipped through the rocks like a blizzard. It scaled the peaks of the solemn, still mountains, rushed amid the primary stones darkened by the foliage and hastened the slow, crystalline summer rivers. Not only did the tumbler fall, so too did the ashtray, a porcelain ashtray shaped like a banana leaf, a gift from one of his old fans. A lot of crumpled cigarette ends were scattered about like tiny scorched trunks.

Summoned by the call were birds that took long migratory flights, little fish that licked the sides of rocks, regally horned deer, and vigilant crows; crocodiles extended their long heads, and the trees seemed to sway. It was a triumphal roar, a key heeded by large pachyderms, haughty flamingos, elusive mollusks. Then,

Jane – tan and glistening – raised her head, moved by the roar as if by a long-awaited provocation. And Jane ran, ran along the jungle trails, fighting her way through the big, fleshy-leaved branches; guided by the roar, protected by the roar, encouraged by the roar, Jane traveled the moist corridors of the jungle. The birds flew after her, the lions hid, the vipers concealed their heads, the great hippopotami gave way.

Not only did the ashtray shatter on the floor: a picture in the bedroom shook; it seemed to bang against the wall and after quivering for a moment in the air (dense with smoke and alcohol), it came to a rest, crooked, yearning, out-of-kilter. It was the full-color copy of an old still of the jungle, of the prefabricated jungle of Lake Toluca, with its cardboard mountains, baobab wallpaper, and swimming pools turned into lakes brimming with piranhas. Outside the apartment, the automobiles making their way down the avenue were alarmed by the roar and came to a halt, but then hastily continued on their way. The elephants shook their huge ears like slow fans; high above, the monkeys traversed the jungle, leaping from one branch to the next; the birds snapped their wings like whips against the fronds of the tall banana trees. In the picture there was also a girl in tiger skins, lying on the ground, chained, her swollen breasts rising from between the dark spots of the tiger, her pale thighs (thighs of someone who takes little sun) visible between the orderly tears in her skirt, her thick, ruddy lips half-opened in what could be a provocative gesture of pain or a sensual entreaty. Johnny was a few steps behind – his broad, muscular torso naked, his chiseled nose, his graceful bones, the small suggestive shadows around his nipples and waist; just above the navel, the beginning of a line, a shapely crease concealed by the triangular loincloth (long between the legs but narrow on

28

the sides, perhaps to highlight the contours of his formidable muscles), but the course of which – like a flowing river – could be imagined.

The picture, based on a scene from *Tarzan and the Amazons* starring him and Brenda Joyce, had been painted by one of his fans, many years ago. From what he could remember of the movie, there was an extraordinary number of girls, arrow bearers, all decked out in sandals fashioned from vines and in tiger skins (discovering that the black spots on the fabric were really the result of an excellent studio dye-job had enraged him; but lions were scarce, at least in Hollywood, and in any case an unbelievable number of advocacy societies for what-have-you – dogs, tigers, even whales – had cropped up, making cinematography a difficult art form). In the movie, he projected his long, sharp, penetrating roar, a roar of the jungle and the mountains, of the water, wood, and wind; a roar that ululated like the foghorn of a Mississippi paddlewheeler, that made the bluebirds of Nork-Fold flap their wings, that attracted salamanders from the swamps of West Palm *(West of the Colorado River there's a place I love . . .)*, and encouraged the ducks of Wisconsin to fly. Johnny roared; he roared on the slopes of the bison-skin couch, and the deer head on the wall didn't move; he roared again, thinking of Maureen O'Sullivan, and the roar thundered across the room like a heavy rock falling on the reefs of Leyte: the madreporic island reproduced the roar in the whisky tumbler that bore the marks of lips and cigarettes and in the Caribbean conch shells, keepsakes in whose cavities the raucous notes of the phosphorescent sea united with the shrill notes of his roar. Johnny roared across the velvety animals of the African blankets that covered the empty double bed of his California apartment, he roared across the ivory curios and the

29

tobacco leaves – a long, desperate, dislocated roar, the roar of a humble receptionist at Caesar's Palace in Vegas, where he'd held his last job, and for a moment he thought that Jane would come, that Jane would cross the snarled central streets, that she would make her way through the shining traffic lights and the glistening metal of the automobiles, that Jane, wearing a leopard-skin overcoat, would cross the neon-sparkling avenue, hurdle the river of peanuts and little bags of popcorn, run through the billboards announcing porno flicks and American Noble Savage cigarettes, and reach the humble apartment where Edgar Rice Burroughs was drinking whisky before he dialed the Retired Actors' Retreat in Woodland Hills, because the roars of an old man named Johnny Weissmuller wouldn't let the neighbors sleep.

The Session

At four o'clock in the afternoon, my psychoanalyst called. Having just discovered his wife's second lover, he was very upset.

'It's unbelievable!' he shouted. 'I won't have it.'

'Calm down,' I advised him. 'Bodies don't exist. People don't either. In reality, we can only talk about functions. Are you with me? None of us is who we think we are, not in relation to ourselves or in relation to others. So, your wife's second lover. . . .'

'I don't want to hear about him!' he yelled, out of sorts. 'I haven't been able to eat since I found out about them. I haven't had a bite all day.'

'That means you can't accept reality. Food has come to represent what you reject. . . .'

'I know,' he whimpered, almost bursting into tears.

'No one dies from not eating for a day or two. The diet will do you good, you'll eliminate toxins.'

'I don't understand why she has to see him on Tuesdays,' he confided more calmly.

I took advantage of the pause to try to put reality into a glass, which is a tricky maneuver. I'd been working at that since dawn, but each time I tried to grasp it, reality slipped away from me. Now, as I spoke over the phone with my psychoanalyst, I tried to hold the glass, reality, and the receiver all at the same time.

'What happens on Tuesdays?' I asked as I pushed the glass toward the center of the nightstand.

'Nothing in particular,' he said. 'It's just that she sees her second lover on that day, and not on any other. I don't understand, why does it have to be on Tuesdays?'

'It's probably the only day they both have free,' I reasoned plainly.

'Far from it,' he corrected me. 'Tuesdays are very complicated. In the morning he gives his philosophy class, at twelve he has lunch with his children, and at six he has his weekly meeting at the university auditorium. As for her, on Tuesdays we have breakfast together, after which she does some yoga and attends her anthropology course, and at night she sings in the Friends of the Baroque choir. Tuesdays are hectic. She should have chosen Saturday. On Saturdays, I visit my mother, the children are out, and he doesn't have any classes to teach.'

I detest the word *classes*, which may explain why at that precise moment reality slid down the legs of the nightstand. As I continued speaking with my psychoanalyst, I attempted to bend over and pick up reality. He must have realized I was up to something, because he suddenly became annoyed.

'But you aren't listening to me,' he snapped.

'Of course I am. I hear you,' I said in my defense. 'Don't be so impatient. Let's try to analyze your feelings of anxiety about this new guy. . . .'

'Don't mention him!' he repeated. 'I find his very existence intolerable, I can't accept it. I don't want to know anything about him. He's disturbing my peace of mind. He's an intruder. Besides, what would the first one say? I can't understand why one lover wasn't enough for her. After all, we're talking about a good kid –

intelligent, serious-minded, even handsome. She has no right to do this to him. I'm certain he has no idea about any of this. We might have even come to be friends – although I hate chemistry, which is his specialty.'

'Wasn't it botany?' I asked innocently, holding the glass in one hand and the receiver in the other. Reality was hiding under the bed. I had to squat in a way that neither he nor reality would notice.

'Botany, chemistry – it makes no difference,' he said. 'One of those horrible scientific fields that explains the world superficially. She adores simple explanations. The description of a tricotyledonus is enough to seduce her.' With great difficulty, I managed to bend my knees. 'To add insult to injury,' he continued, 'the world is full of tricotyledonuses.'

'But according to you,' I stated, not wanting to lose ground (by then I was almost on my knees), 'he's a professor of philosophy.'

'She believes that philosophy is a branch of chemistry,' he remarked bitterly. 'And now don't try telling me that that's proof of her intelligence, because I won't accept that.'

'There are too many things you're unwilling to accept, my friend,' I countered firmly. On my knees, I was able to look under the bed. 'The question is, are you in a position not to accept?'

Cunningly, he evaded my question. 'I don't understand why she couldn't make do with the first one,' he said, whimpering once again. 'It'll come as such a blow to him. The poor guy is really in love. And at the moment, he's working on a very difficult essay – about the effect of laser beams on frog pepsins. He won't be able to take this blow.'

On the floor – I was down on my knees – I found two cigarette butts, an empty matchbox, and a sock I'd lost the day before. But reality remained in hiding, camouflaged by dust.

I tried to console him. 'It's always possible he'll never find out.'

'True, just like parents are the last ones to find out what their children are up to,' he admitted. 'But if they do something careless, like take a stroll arm in arm, or show up at the movies at the same time. . . .'

'People no longer stroll arm in arm,' I said. 'In reality, I don't think people stroll at all these days. As for the movies, it's very dark in the theaters. I suppose it's possible the three of them might run into one another before the lights are turned off. It would be a matter of slipping away in time.'

'I don't think she would,' he replied. 'She's an exhibitionist. For example, she loves to go to the movies with me, even though there's always the possibility that lover number one might see us together. That's why I prefer to go in after the movie has started.'

'The movie has always begun,' I argued subtly, as I thought to myself, *now I'll catch it!* I'd seen reality under the bed, behind an old shoe.

'I hate beginnings almost as much as endings,' he confided. 'In reality, I'm only interested in what comes in the middle. That's where everything acquires depth. Apart from that, the ending can always be found within a good beginning, which only undermines the dénouement. But the middle can develop in so many ways.'

Either it wasn't an old shoe or it wasn't reality, because I couldn't grasp either, not in any case without letting go of the receiver.

'I notice that your voice sounds faint at times. What are you doing?' he demanded to know.

'It's the telephone exchange,' I lied. 'There's interference on the line.'

'There's always interference on the line,' he said, categorically.

34

'It has to do with the tension,' I added.

'A physical problem,' he argued.

'Impossible to control from a room,' I stated.

'Especially if the room is shuttered and dark.'

'And no one has opened the windows.'

'Because there's something unbearable about light.'

'The specks of dust that you begin to see, like an invasion of mysterious, sparkling, hungry particles.'

'Last night, she came in through that door,' he sobbed, 'and she wasn't with the usual man. She was with the other one.'

'And you were afraid because you didn't know him.'

'She'd never introduced me to him before.'

'But his face was vaguely familiar.'

'Yes, it was vaguely familiar, like the face in a dream I had as a child.'

'And you didn't know what to say to him.'

'I held out my hand. This hand. Then I rushed to wash it. I apologized. I felt I was annoying them.'

'On how many previous occasions would you say you've been annoying?'

'I think I've always been a slight annoyance, like something out of kilter. My hand is too cold or else it's sweaty, my tone of voice is one note lower or higher than it should be, I make the witty remark a moment too soon or a moment too late. And then she comes in with this other guy.'

'Into the dark room.'

'I couldn't bring myself to turn on the light.'

'The invading particles.'

'Or even to say, "Go away!" '

'Every act has its consequences.'

35

'To be avoided, if possible.'

'To refuse to act is to refuse to accept the consequences.'

'The other party would commit the act anyway.'

'Audaciously.'

'Boldly. I hate his courage.'

'Which exists in relation to its opposite.'

'There are no people, just functions.'

'And submissiveness, which presupposes the existence of an authority.'

'Of power.'

'In the face of which there are only two possibilities: rebellion or slavery. Which are interchangeable. Little by little, the hunter becomes the prey. And the prey, the hunter.'

'That's a very sound observation. Ah, it's 4:50 now. Your session is over,' my psychoanalyst decreed in his typical fashion. 'I'll see you again tomorrow afternoon. Remember, if for any reason you can't attend, my secretary will charge you anyway. Goodbye.'

When I heard him hang up, I rushed to look under the bed. I thought I saw reality slithering across the wall. Like a tiny, dark patch of dust.

The Lizard Christmas

I got up early to go hunt lizards. With my black stick that has a stone at the end of it. It hasn't rained for nine months, and it still isn't raining. If it doesn't rain before the Baby is born in the manger at the church, we probably won't have Christmas or New Year's, or any year. The years will come to a standstill, turn to stone, and stop going by. We'll be stuck in this age forever and I won't grow and we'll die children, thirsty and dust-covered, wither away, dry up like the fields, the plants, the grass. And the Baby won't be born either, even though the road is full of lizards warming themselves in the sun, sleeping in the drowsy heat on a bed of dry earth, on earth so dry there isn't a shriveled up plant or a miserable little tree in sight. But I like the heat.

From the bottom of the dry well, my grandfather calls me an evil dunce because I'm happy about the heat. He went down to the bottom of the well to wait for water. It hasn't started raining yet, but on a lot of afternoons the sky is full of gray clouds, some of which are unusually dark and black on the top; they gather above the hill, the pitiful yellow hill. That's when we all think it's going to rain, that finally the water will fall. Women rush to put pots outside. With their pans ready, they look at the sky, waiting for the first drops to fall, and we all think that my grandfather will finally come out of the well. He made a vow, I'm going into the well, he said, several days ago, and I won't come out until the water forces me out, until the water begins to rise in the well, until birds are reflected in it as they fly through the air.

And the evil heat makes the lizards come out, leave the hill for the bed of the dry river (whose name no one remembers) where the thirsty, tired cows with nothing to drink or chew on go and lie down. I stalk the lizards. I hide, and when they come out I aim right at the center of their heads. I close one eye so I won't miss, the stones go flying (like prehistoric birds, my stones are the only things that fly through the hot, dry air) and smash their round, brown, pupil-less heads. For every five lizards I catch, the leather trader pays one peso. But the lizards don't come out every day. The sun has to be really hot for them to leave the scrub, you have to wait for them to come out from the holes where they spend the winter. Because they like the heat. So when the sun beats down, they come plodding – slowly, heavily, as if lugging a rigid carcass – across the dry grass until they find a place that's boiling hot where they can stretch out and bake under the sun.

I got up early and went to the hill. When I walked past the well, I peeked down at my grandfather, at my grandfather who sits down there at the bottom of the dry well waiting for the rains to come. While walking by I made a little noise with my stick so he would know I was there. He heard me and, at the top of his lungs – as if the rim of the well were a distant mountain peak – he asked me how the sky was looking. To make him feel better, I told him there were some big black clouds in the sky. 'What direction are they coming from?' the old man asked, a little more gently. I looked to one extreme and then another of the clear, shimmering, empty sky and said, 'From the north. The fat clouds full of water are coming from the north.'

'Good, that means they're *verendas*,' said Grandfather, who liked to christen things.

He waits for rain and the lizards wait for sun. A lot of lizards have been leaving their holes recently. Slow and lazy, they drag themselves across the land; then they lie down, endlessly still, as if they were made of stone, to feel the heat. I wait for them. And the Virgin waits for the Baby. The local Virgin is my neighbor. She wasn't always a Virgin: this is her first time. I didn't know she was the Virgin, but yesterday, when I went into the church to see the manger, I discovered she was the Virgin, so I immediately got down on my knees. They were setting up the shelter, and Joseph was arranging the hay. There was an empty cradle where I thought they'd put the Child as soon as he was born. And there she was, silent, wearing a long dress I'd never seen on her before, with a shawl over her head; she was arranging the flowers and helping prepare the house. It was dark in the church, but I could see her clearly. There were people around and you could hear a lot of murmuring because, with the shortage of water, everyone was going to the church, everyone except my grandfather who had climbed down into the well. She looked very tall, taller than when from the back of my house I see her strolling among the sunflowers or reaching for an apple. Joseph was speaking to her, but I couldn't hear what he was saying. Up above, where two poles at the top of the lean-to met at a sharp angle, there was an enormous, glittering star. I thought the shawl was very pretty, but I prefer to see her with her hair down. Then she sat down on the wooden bench, next to the cradle of the baby that still hadn't arrived, and remained there motionless, her big blue eyes looking straight ahead. Right then, the stick I always carry around fell, the stick with a stone at its tip. I had to lean over to pick it up, and she looked at me. I was a little embarrassed about the noise the stick had made when it fell, but she smiled at me so I moved a little closer to her and asked, 'When will the Baby be born?'

'Tomorrow,' she answered. 'The Coming will be tomorrow.'

Since I was a little nervous, I ran off to the hill, which was baking hot. When I got there, I started throwing stones at the trees because I didn't see any lizards.

Today I woke up thinking that this will be the day the Baby arrives, and, when he does, maybe a little rain will arrive too. Everyone will leave presents at the foot of His cradle. Because He's not just any baby. And she will be there, waiting to rock Him. So at the crack of dawn I went to the hill to see if some early-rising lizard would feel like coming out, coming out to find me waiting for it, waiting with the black stick with a stone at the tip. If the lizard is really sleepy, I don't have to aim at it from a long way away; I can just smash its head with the stick. And I was lucky, because as soon as I got to the hill and started rolling some cornhusk cigarettes, I noticed that off in the distance, two big, sleepy, sundrenched lizards were crawling out, slow and heavy. I like being out in the sun, so I waited patiently. There wasn't a single cloud on the horizon and the cicadas, drunken from the light, were singing. With all the heat, the village is full of flies and so is the hill. They're blue and buzz all over the place, and if you stand still, they get in your eyes and nose. The smoke scares them away, so I blew the smoke from the cornhusks right at them. Slowly, the lizards started moving. The Baby would have a lot of presents. In spite of the heat, the drought, the cloudless sky, his arrival would be celebrated. And He might have more presents than ever, to persuade Him to make it rain. Everyone in the village, the three wise men, people from different places will come to welcome the

40

Baby. And she will be there, motionless, looking at the cradle. One of the lizards lay down on the side of the hill, next to a stone that was bleached by the sun, and remained there like a statue. The lizard barely flinched when I clobbered it with the stick. The sun was in my face, little rays of light got in between my eyelashes, and I tried to brush them away with my hand. Not far away, the other lizard was sprawled out amid the dry weeds. I came up from behind and aimed carefully at the center of its stubby head. Its skin was hot, like the skin of someone who's spent too much time in the sun. Carrying the two lizards, I made my way down the hill to the drunken squeal of the cicadas. The cicadas are in the branches, singing because there's a lot of sun, clamoring among the pinecones that open and release their transparent, white-winged seeds. It's as hard to see them as it is to avoid hearing them. On the way, I found other little lizards, but I didn't pay any attention to them. I walked fast and when I reached the village I went to the church.

There were a lot of people at the door, like every time there's a ceremony. I was thinking about my grandfather at the bottom of the well. From down there, he couldn't see I'd lied about the clouds, but he must have realized by then. At the door to the church, people couldn't seem to make up their minds whether to go in or keep on looking sadly at the bright sky, at the fact that the sun was round and merciless. Tired of the heat, they finally went in. I went in too, but through the little door, the one that's partly broken and the priest is always trying to get donations for so he can fix it. I pushed gently, because it could break at any moment. I could make out the big manger displayed over to one side, with hay scattered around the floor, a bright star up above, Joseph's tools (he's a carpenter), the wooden cradle, and, finally, the Virgin wearing a long dress, with a shawl over her head. I walked toward her slowly, without making any noise because the church, despite all the people, was silent, sort of solemn. It was very dark, but candles flickered in the stable where people were waiting for the Baby.

I could make out red apples, oranges, big ripe lemons, and a tethered goat at the foot of the cradle.

From one side, without her noticing me, I approached the Virgin. She looked straight ahead and had a very calm expression on her face; she was composed, dignified. Before, I'd seen her walk around in the yard, whitewash the walls, pick up lemons from the ground, pluck a chicken for lunch. And back then I didn't know she was the Virgin. Back then we spoke like neighbors. She asked about my grandfather, my mother, I told her our dog had died.

I went up to her and silently dropped the lizards in her skirt. She was a little surprised to feel their weight. She withdrew her gaze from where it had been fixed (where had those fishlike eyes of hers been swimming?), but in the semidarkness she might not have seen me. She looked at the dead lizards. I stood very still in a dark corner. The Baby hadn't been born yet: the cradle was empty. But she was waiting for Him.

'I want to be the Baby' I said in the darkness, speaking softly. 'Please, let me be the Baby.'

The lizards were there in her skirt, as motionless as when they sun themselves on the road. They look the same when they're dead as when they're asleep.

The lizards were a small dark spot on her skirt.

Not having seen me yet in the darkness, she said, 'The offerings for the Baby must be offerings of life, not death. Spare them today, on the day of the Arrival. Nothing dead should be around

42

His cradle. Everything should be breathing, fresh, do you understand? She straightened her back a bit. She was sitting on the wooden bench at the foot of the Baby's cradle. Grabbing the lizards by the tail, she looked for me in the darkness.

'They aren't for Him,' I responded, furious. 'I didn't catch them for the Baby. He gets everything, they're for you,' I said, rebelliously. 'I can bring you more, as many as you want. For five of them, the leather man pays a peso. I can go up on the hill whenever you want and get more. Hold onto them and by nighttime, when the sun has set, you'll have a lot of lizards, a lot of skins to sell to the man who pays. . . .'

'Today, we're paying tribute to Him.' she said. 'For the newborn. For Him, the one who will arrive. Take your lizards and offer them to Him, or better still: in His name, spare their lives.'

Left with no alternative, I grabbed the lizards and bolted out of the church. I didn't know where I was going, but on the way I passed by the well where my grandfather was holding out. I tossed the lizards on the ground, grabbed the rope, and slid my way down to the bottom of the well. In candlelight, grandfather was grumbling curses about life. He wasn't surprised to see me at the bottom of the well.

'It was about time you came down here,' he told me, unsmiling. 'Start banging on those cans,' he added. 'Sometimes that brings rain.'

The Crack

The man hesitated as he climbed the stairs that led from one subway platform to another. As a result of his momentary irresolution (he didn't know whether he should proceed or wait, go forward or backward – in fact, he didn't know whether he'd been going down or up), serious turmoil broke out. The dense mass of people behind him broke the intricate yet casual mesh of time and space, scattering like an exploding star that ushers in a diaspora of light or an eclipse. Bewildered men slipped, women screamed, children were trampled, an old man lost his wig and a lady her false teeth, a street vendor's goods were scattered about, someone seized the opportunity to steal some magazines from a kiosk, there was a case of attempted rape, a wristwatch flew through the air, and several women accidentally exchanged handbags.

The man was subsequently arrested and accused of disturbing the peace. He too had suffered the consequences of his own indiscretion: in the confusion, he'd broken a tooth. It was ascertained that at the precise moment the incident occurred, the man who hesitated on the stairs that led from one platform to another (eighty feet below ground where there is artificial light day and night) had been in position three of line fifteen – to the extent that positions and lines can be established in reference to people going up and down stairs.

The interrogation took place on a cold, damp afternoon during the month of November. The man asked to know which equinox had last occurred; as a result of his hesitation, which had led to the accident, his ideas about the world were in a state of disarray.

'It's winter, of course,' the civil servant in charge of the interrogation answered with evident disdain.

'I didn't mean to offend you,' the man said timidly. 'I can't tell you how grateful I am for your kind reply,' he added.

'Leaving winter aside,' the civil servant softened his tone, 'could you explain to me the cause of this unfortunate incident?'

The man looked at one green wall, then another. When he'd entered the building, they had seemed gray to him; but like so many other things, it must have been a false impression – unless of course, at some moment they were to become gray again. Who knows what the future will bring?

'Well, sir,' he cleared his throat. He didn't see a glass of water anywhere and it seemed inappropriate to request one. Perhaps it was better not to ask for anything. Not even for understanding. Bare, windowless walls. Rectangular, but narrow, rooms.

The civil servant seemed slightly annoyed. That's how he *seemed*. He'd never seen a civil servant who hadn't seemed annoyed. It was something like an occupational hazard or a bad habit one picks up from living with someone.

'All of a sudden,' said the man, 'I didn't know whether to go forward or not. I know perfectly well that this is strange. It's strange to have a thought like that while going up or down the stairs. Or perhaps even while doing anything at all.'

'What step were you on?' the civil servant asked, with professional coldness.

'I can't say for certain,' the man answered truthfully. 'I'd like

45

to find out. I'm certain someone must know. Some people always count the steps, in either direction, whether they're coming or going.'

'And you? Were you coming or going?'

'I was undecided. Slightly hesitant. Do you know what I mean?' Suddenly, as his gaze once again moved across the green surface of the wall, the man spotted a tiny opening, an almost imperceptible crack. He didn't know whether the crack had been there when he'd looked at the wall for the first or second time, or whether it had opened up at that very moment. Because there must have been a time when the wall was completely smooth – gray or green, with no cracks in it. And how would he know when that little fissure had appeared? In any case, it was very awkward not to know whether it was an ancient crack or a modern one. He looked at it intently, trying to understand it.

'My question still stands,' the civil servant insisted in a tone of indolent severity. He had to proceed as if he were dealing with a child. Remain patient. That's what the instructors said. It was an old but effective system. Repetition leads to success by means of wear and tear. Repetition destroys. 'What step were you on?'

The man thought the crack seemed a little wider, but he didn't know if it was an optical illusion or if it had really grown. In any case, he said to himself, at some point it will grow, it's a question of paying attention, or perhaps of not paying attention.

'I couldn't say for certain,' said the man. 'Are there any optical illusions in this room?'

The civil servant did not *appear* surprised. In fact, functionaries almost never appear surprised by anything, which is part of their function.

'No,' he said in a flat voice. 'Were you coming or going?'

'Someone must know,' the man replied, his gaze fixed on the wall. So it was possible the crack had grown at that very moment, grown silently in the green darkness, like a malignant cell with an intention that differed from that of all the other cells.

'Why not you?' the civil servant asked.

'It all happened so fast,' the man said aloud, although not addressing the civil servant in particular. He was trying to describe the phenomenon accurately.

The hole in the wall looked harmless, but that was probably just an illusion.

'I suppose I was going down, or up, it's all the same. There were stairs ahead of me and stairs behind. It was so crowded I couldn't see the steps until they were right below my feet. There were so many of us. A vague awareness of being part of the horde. I went through the motions mechanically, like always.'

'Were you going up or down?' the civil servant repeated in a tone of routine patience. The man felt it was a case of impersonal deference, a duty on the part of the functionary whose patience was not directed specifically at him. It was a professional habit, not precisely a good habit.

'We're talking about a single staircase,' said the man, 'that can lead either up or down. It all depends on the decision one took previously. The steps are all the same: cement, gray, the same width. I experienced a minor hesitation. In the middle of the staircase, with throngs in front of me and throngs behind, I was actually uncertain whether I was going up or down. I don't know if you can understand what having that tiny doubt means, sir. It's a type of confusion. Either I was going up or I was going down – which, in part, was the basis of my hesitation – and suddenly I didn't know what to do. My right foot remained suspended in the air for a moment. The significance of the act was painfully clear to me. I couldn't put my foot down until I knew how to rest it. It was, therefore, necessary to resolve that uncertainty.'

The crack in the wall was the size of a small coin. But before it had looked no larger than the head of a pin. Or was it that, before, he hadn't realized its true size? The difficulty in grasping reality lies in the concept of time, he thought. In the absence of continuity, you have to accept that no reality exists aside from the present. The *present.* Like that precise moment when, uncertain whether he was going up or down, it had been impossible to rest his foot. Above the crack he could now make out a thin, wavy line leading upward – if one looked at it from below – or downward – if one looked at it from above. The direction was determined, in this instance, by the level at which the eye was situated.

'Perhaps you recall,' the civil servant suggested, almost gently, 'whether you were going up or down the stairs at the instant immediately preceding the incident you are recounting.'

'It's odd that the same instrument is good for going up and down – at heart two antithetical actions,' the man thought aloud. 'The stairs are more worn toward the middle, where we step – whether we're going up or down. I thought that if I rested my foot, I would only deepen the indentation. A moment before hesitating,' he continued, 'a gap opened in my memory. Memory can drift, spring a leak. Mine got stuck in the underground, it was no use.'

'According to your charts,' the civil servant interrupted forcefully, 'you'd never suffered from amnesia before.'

'No,' the man stated. 'It's a literary device. It was an unexpected crack.'

The line rose in the direction of the ceiling. Only with effort

48

could he follow it because he had difficulty seeing something that far away. When submerged, only an abstraction allows us to know whether the current is taking us to the source or the outlet of the river, to where it begins or ends.

'A moment before the accident,' the civil servant repeated, 'were you going up or down?'

'It was just a brief hesitation. Going up? Going down? I had my foot . . . in the air . . . I was about to put it down, and suddenly: *uncertainty*. There was nothing dramatic about it, there was just a kind of confusion. Placing my foot on the step would represent a decisive act. I held it in the air for a few moments. It was an uncomfortable but less definitive position.'

'What type of hesitation was it?' asked the civil servant, irate. He was either fed up or had changed tactics. The crack branched off in different directions. No one's perfect. It wasn't clear whether those ramifications led somewhere.

'Given my uncertainty, I didn't act,' the man confessed. 'It seemed wiser to wait, wait until my foot could once again resume its duty without any confusion, until my leg would no longer ask inadmissible questions.'

'What type of hesitation was it?' the civil servant repeated gruffly.

'It was the derivative sort. Class G. Considered dangerous. There's no need to check the catalog, sir,' said the man, defeated. 'A hesitation with ramifications. The sort that comes with a family, as a result of which it's no longer a question of determining if you're going up or down the stairs: it doesn't matter, that's meaningless. So the people behind you – whether you're going up or down there's always a horde ahead of you and another in back – knock into one another, accidentally. Some people yell, everyone demands to know what's happening, the sirens wail, the walls shake and crack, children cry, ladies lose buttons and umbrellas, the inspectors meet, and civil servants investigate the irregularity.' The crack was extending like the ripple that follows a fish. 'Could you give me a cigarette?'

The Rebellious Sheep

Everything would be easier if that sheep out in front would finally jump. The nights are long, the pasture very green. The city is dark.

Looking absently to one side, it doesn't jump. I stop to examine its gaze. It's their eyes that tell us animals are different. The sheep refuses to jump. The last café to close shuts its doors at three. As I leave the place, the trees are very still. The odd car speeds down the street with a freedom it would lack during the day. I'd never thought about sheep until it occurred to me to count them. It seemed like a simple enough procedure. It's the stillness, the silence and loneliness of the night, that keeps me awake. My steps, which I'd prefer not to hear, in the coldness of my house. The stairs creak as I go up, the echo of rheumatic wood. Those are the bones, the bones of the city that can be heard at that hour when everyone is asleep and that sheep, the one in the front of the flock, refuses to jump. I close my eyes. In the darkness of my pupils, I can make out a green field, a white fence, a flock of motionless sheep. Indifferently, they look from one side to the other, as if looking were unimportant. Then I try to force the one in front to move. With my eyes closed, I concentrate on the act of ordering the sheep to jump over the fence. I don't know how a man whose eyes are closed but who isn't asleep can make himself be obeyed. I get annoyed with myself. Why does that stubborn sheep refuse to follow orders? I try to think about something else but it doesn't work. From out of the solitude of my closed eyelids, in the darkness of the night, I have summoned the sheep, and now that it has appeared, with its thick coat of wool, stubby ears, and feigned passivity, I can't get rid of it. How is it that our roles have come to be reversed? I have the urge to shout, *I'm the one in charge.* But it would remain indifferent to that shout too. It doesn't hear me. The one in front isn't always the same one. But only an expert can tell one sheep from another, especially if your eyes are shut, if there's no light in the room, if the city is dark, if the trees aren't moving, if the phone isn't ringing. As a matter of fact, the only thing I can say about the sheep in front is that it's in front. Nothing distinguishes it from the others except that it's near the white fence and that, if I'm ever going to fall asleep, I have to get that one to jump. If I could get it to jump, it's likely the others would follow suit. I'm *sure* they would. They wouldn't offer the slightest resistance, they would do what the one before them had done, and then I could count them as they jump over the fence, one at a time. Then, gently, sleep would come to me, sleep mixed with clouds, fleece, pasture, and a steadily ascending tally. But the stubborn one out in front won't budge. Sometimes it gets close to the fence, but only to uproot some grass. It doesn't look up and shows no interest in what's on the other side. Sometimes I think it feels it would be stupid to jump, that jumping is something that would only occur to a tired, feeble man who can't fall asleep. When it comes right down to it, why would it want to jump? From what it can tell, the field on the other side is exactly the same. The grass is no different over there, and the prospect of straying from the flock doesn't appeal to it. 'Come on now, let's go, little sheep,' I tell it. 'Aren't you interested in the unknown?' It doesn't look at me. As a matter of fact, not only can I not get it to jump, I can't even get it to look at me. As far as it's concerned, I don't think I exist. But the sheep and all its infuriating stubbornness are real enough for me. I have to accept my rebellious little sheep. In considering people whose sheep jump over the fence every night I conclude they must be better shepherds than I am. My flock is indifferent. It doesn't feel the thrill of risk, isn't tempted by adventure. The white wall is the accepted limit of its universe.

'Don't you think the wall is a form of oppression?' I sometimes ask the sheep out in front. It doesn't answer. Without a worry in the world, the motionless sheep gazes off to one side. The wall, therefore, isn't a barrier. The fact that my sheep won't jump gives me a rare distinction. It means I am not their owner. I'm not in charge of the vigil that keeps me from falling asleep. I have no hope of falling asleep.

'The sheep refuses to jump,' I told a colleague from the office one night. We were at my house, playing chess. As a simple procedure for falling asleep he had recommended I count sheep as they jump over the white fence. He raised his eyes from the board (holding in his hand a lethal knight). Unruffled (the man is not easily surprised), he asked me, 'Which one?'

'The one in front,' I replied.

He placed his knight in a position that would doubtless lead to my demise. I don't know how to counterattack so, even if I'm winning, this sends me plummeting into defeat.

'Force it,' he advised dramatically.

I can only win when I'm playing against myself, when my right hand is playing against my left hand.

That night, exasperated at having lost again despite having been ahead and having taken one more piece than he had, I decided to force the rebellious sheep. As soon as I went to bed, I shut my eyes and made the field appear and the sheep graze. It was the same old field and the same flock. One sheep, not far from the others, was grazing near the fence. 'Jump!' I ordered dictatorially. The sheep didn't budge, didn't even raise its head. 'Jump!' I said again, and I think my voice echoed in the silence of the building, across the dark city. 'Jump, damn you!' I repeated. It didn't hear my shout. It went on grazing near the fence, without looking up.

Then I armed myself with a stick. I don't know where I found it because I don't tend to keep weapons in the house. I hate violence. Brandishing the stick, I approached the sheep, the one in front. It didn't seem to see me, or if it did the stick didn't mean anything to it. I shook the stick in the air, above the sheep's curly nape. My first blow landed on the sheep's head, between the ears, and I seemed to be squashing something soft, probably thick curls of wool. Then, slowly, the sheep turned its soft, dark eyes toward me. 'Jump!' I yelled, exasperated. But once it had turned around, the fence was behind it. Its black eyes were now trained on me, but despite my fury the word fence meant nothing to the sheep. How is it possible that it couldn't understand such a simple command? 'Jump!' I shouted again, and landed a second blow, hard and furious, on the same spot. This time the sheep retreated, staggering, its back to the white fence. We were separated from the group, face to face: the other sheep were grazing, the pasture was green, beyond the fence lay another identical field. Was there any reason for it to jump? 'Jump!' I said again, and with the third blow a trickle of blood began to wet its curly fleece. Looking at it, the blood mixed with wool, excited me. There were pieces of leaves and twigs tangled in the curls. I felt the urge to remove them, to pet the sheep, and also to kill it. 'Why the hell don't you jump,

54

you damn sheep?' I shouted. This time I struck the sheep's soft, fluffy back. That sheep was going to die an unnatural death one day, but for now it was content to graze, to chew the cud along with the others, even if doing so meant I'd never fall asleep, that sleep would be denied me forever because making the sheep jump was the only way to get what I wanted. Bees, dark leaves, and tiny stems were tangled in its fleece. The dark, viscous blood stained the wool slightly. The other sheep were grazing.

The animal looked at me, failing to understand what I wanted. The fence was behind it, a simple, harmless white fence that could be jumped over easily if the sheep would only try. 'You can do it, jump!' I shouted as I hit it again on the back. Something seemed to crack, but it wasn't the floorboards or the fence. The sheep continued to retreat; now it was a few steps away. To hit it again, I had to move toward it, something I found revolting. Why was it so stubborn? If it would only realize, if it were capable of understanding what I was asking for; its legs quivered, and with each blow the animal seemed more defenseless. 'Now it'll bend its legs,' I thought. It's going to lie down on the ground until it bleeds to death, until it dies, but it won't jump, it won't go over the fence and make the others follow it.

The stick was stained, and looking at it excited me. 'That's the only way to deal with you,' I told the sheep. Then I plunged the stick into its belly, taking advantage of the fact that the animal was on its side. I didn't know sheep had pink bellies. I'm a man of the city, I'm not used to looking at sheep, admiring their undersides, oh, such a soft belly. The sheep was heaving its last breath, it was going to die at any moment, without having jumped. I hit it again, this time in the pink area, hit its soft flesh, its tender sheep flesh that would no longer make it to the slaughterhouse because the sheep hadn't jumped, because it didn't know that the fence was a surmountable obstacle. As I sank the stick into its soft underside for the last time I trembled and was overcome with drowsiness. I was happy. In its flesh, its warm pale flesh that I was now touching with my eager hands, the stick was still. And it was that warmth, that gentle contact that made me drowsy, and I knew I was going to fall asleep. Stained with blood, clinging to the sheep's ravaged but still warm entrails, I was going to fall asleep, like an innocent child who still hasn't jumped over the white fence.

Deaf as a Doorknob

The door was made of solid oak, but the passage of time and a certain amount of abuse were evident in the scars and in two deep wrinkles around the peephole. It might be worth adding that that lone eye in the middle, at the center of the forehead, was small for such a big door. But no one's perfect. The door had been varnished. There's always someone willing to varnish a door. The coat might have been applied to celebrate some anniversary, someone might have looked at the door and said, 'This door could use a coat of varnish' (some women could use a hat, a beauty mark, or a new pair of sandals), or maybe, while clearing the dishes, the lady of the house had looked at her husband and said, 'If we're having your family over for the birthday party, you'd better start varnishing the door.' Or else, home alone one Saturday afternoon, a man, the melancholy owner of the door, might have varnished it to pass the time. However it had happened, when he found the door only a few traces of the coat of varnish remained, gentle streams of oil flowing toward the edges.

He found the door at night in a vacant lot full of cats, surrounded by empty crates, rusty cans, and broken bottles. Someone had burned it with a cigarette (depraved people are always taking advantage of the weak, especially in dark places and if the party concerned is attractive), leaving it with a stigma, a hole in the middle of its body. The dirt and dust could be removed easily enough with a rag, unlike the mark left by the savage hand, which couldn't be covered over easily and wouldn't fade with time.

Exhausted, the door had swooned. And it weighed a lot. He picked it up as best he could. Once he'd managed to stand it on end he heaved a sigh. The door was almost as tall as he was. Before starting to walk, he covered it with a newspaper, which might have made the door look unattractive, but he felt more comfortable that way.

The journey wasn't easy. Sometimes, the door would tip to one side or the other, sometimes it would fall altogether. His back hurt. He noticed a lot of people looking on, but that didn't worry him; at night people are more attentive.

When they made it home, he decided not to take the elevator: he would drag the door up the stairs, at the risk of both of them falling or of waking up the neighbors. On the landing, he leaned the door against the wall and rested. He wiped the sweat from his brow, switched back on the light that had turned itself off, and took just two puffs on his cigarette; he wanted to rest his lungs, at least until he got inside.

As if coming back tipsy from a party, they stumbled the last few steps of the way, the door balanced on his back while he searched for the keys. Eventually, he opened up.

He placed the door flat on the floor and went to look for a rag to clean its wounds with, the bruises from the vacant lot. He removed pieces of moss, cleaned out insect bites and the scratchings of cats. He worked gently, slowly, respectfully. Luckily, none of the wounds were very serious. Then he lifted the door again and leaned it against a wall, next to the window where the light from the streetlamps filtered through. He wanted the door to have a different view from the one it had had in the vacant lot. The door could pass the time watching the swings go back and forth (teenagers smoked grass until dawn in the square) and the comings and goings of stray dogs. Since it was night, the door could look out and see, between the streaks of neon lights, the dark trunks of the linden trees and, with a little effort (which would be possible as soon as the door was feeling better), some distant stars glimmering above a laboratory tower.

He left the door there so it could rest while he did other things. He washed his hands and arms, which were very dirty, put the coffeepot on the stove, brushed the dust off his shoes, lit a cigarette, which he puffed on slowly, watered the fern that sat on the middle of the table. He poured himself some coffee, in a white cup, which was just like the ones in the cafés because he liked some things to be the way they were meant to be.

Then he went back into the dark living room, which was illuminated only by the light from the street that filtered in through the window (the black outlines of the trees, the swings sweeping back and forth across the void, the tower rising above the laboratory, the dogs barking and running, the slap of cars rounding the corner, a nearby radio playing dance music). He looked at the door and spoke to it.

He apologized for the rough trip, for having wrapped it in newspaper (he was very sensitive to orifices, he couldn't stand empty holes). Maybe it wasn't so important after all, they could find another way to solve the problem, maybe by using a piece of cloth as a patch, maybe with plastic surgery. The other things could be corrected with time. The uneven paint could be fixed with some new cosmetics, available in any store. Even if the scars weren't easy to cover, he didn't think they would make much of

59

a difference. They gave it character and maturity, which aren't exactly abundant in this world. As for the cigarette burns, he assured the door he was a peaceful man, he hated violence, and the house was full of ashtrays. All he wanted was to slowly tell it the story of his life.

Full Stop

When we met, she said, 'I'll give you the full stop. It's very valuable – don't lose it. Hold onto it for the right moment. It's the most important thing I can give you; I'm doing this because you've earned my trust – so don't let me down.'

For a long time, I kept the full stop in my pocket. Jumbled up with coins, bits of tobacco, and matches, it got a little dirty. We were so happy I never thought we'd need it. Later I bought a case, where I put it for safekeeping. Free of disappointment and tedium, the days went by blissfully. In the mornings, we would wake up happy, joyful at being together; each day presented us with a vast, unknown world of surprises. Familiar things ceased to be familiar, recovering their newness, while other things, like parks and lakes, became inviting and maternal. We went around the streets noticing things other people didn't see. Aromas, colors, light, time, and space were more intense for us. As if under the effects of a powerful drug, our sense of perception had grown more acute. But we weren't drunk, just perceptive and calm, endowed with an unusual capacity to be in harmony with the world. Our senses sang a unique melody that respected the apparent order of things without submitting to it.

I was feeling so happy I forgot about the case, or else I misplaced it. Who knows? Our happiness is all gone now, and I can't find the full stop anywhere, which makes for conflict and frustration. 'Where did you leave it?' she'll ask me, irate. 'What are you waiting for? Hurry up, otherwise the past will lose its beauty and meaning.'

I search the wardrobes, coats, and drawers, underneath seat cushions, below the table and the bed. But I can't find the full stop anywhere. Or the case. The search has become unnerving, obsessive. Maybe I lost the full stop during one of our happy moments. It isn't in the living room, the bedroom, or the fireplace. Could the cat have eaten it?

Not being able to find the full stop exacerbates the pain and suffering. So long as it's missing, we're chained by links of anger, apathy, shame, and hatred. We're forced to put up with this, to give up the hope of beginning a new life. The nights are terrible – we share a room where anxiety, from floor to ceiling, chokes us like a noxious vapor and stains the furniture, the closets, and the books scattered across the floor. Even though at heart we know the problem is the disappearance of the full stop, which she blames on me, anything can get us into an argument. Sometimes I think she even suspects I have it hidden somewhere, to get back at her for something. 'I shouldn't have trusted you,' she reproaches me. 'I should have known you'd betray me.'

It was a long, silver case, one of those cases that people used to keep snuff in. I got it at a flea market; it seemed like a perfect place for the full stop. The tiny, round stop was very comfortable in there. But so many years have gone by. It might have been lost in a move, or maybe someone stole it, thinking it was valuable.

After searching for it in vain all day I leave the house to avoid her reproachful glare, her hateful voice. All of our former happiness has disappeared, and it's hopeless to think it will come back.

But, we can't break up. That missing full stop binds us to one another, making us angry and frustrated, and one by one devours the beautiful days we once had together.

I only hope that some day, just by chance, it will turn up in some pocket, mixed in with other things. By then it would be a sad, fat, dirty, dusty, inopportune full stop, like the ones used by novice writers.

The Inconclusive Journey

Pandemonium broke out when it was discovered we were on a one-way voyage to nowhere. Screams, pleas, and unanswerable questions were heard, crowds gathered on the deck, scuffles erupted. A culprit was urgently sought. Although it would have been difficult to find one through due process, no one was asking for conclusive evidence; suspicion was enough. But the accused had alibis to satisfy even those souls most intent on finding a scapegoat. The doctor assured us he had been hired to treat colds caused by the stormy weather; the acrobats (there's a traveling circus in our midst) complained, 'If only a few ropes and trapezes were enough to get us across the sea'; the actress, uncertain of the role she was supposed to play this time grew impatient, alternately crying, laughing, and complaining about the absence of a director with clear instructions. But it was no use. When we realized we were on a ship without a course, that would never call at any port, it was already too late.

With food in short supply and the sea getting rough at night, some people, preferring to hasten our cruel, implacable fate, choose to hurl themselves into the water. The sleeping tablets are all gone, but some of the more clever passengers are coming up with schemes for committing suicide. In this atmosphere of general confusion and despair, someone decided to take on the role of captain (we also discovered, only too late, that we were traveling without a crew). He stepped up on a platform on the deck and called for silence. Only the waves refused to be quiet. Then he said, 'Compañeros!' (There was a collective shudder. For reasons not worth explaining now, the word sent shivers down the spines of two types of people.)

'Compañeros,' he repeated, this time less emphatically. (Is he a student of political science, or just an enthusiast? I wondered.)

'What is happening to us . . .'

(Faint whispers all about. Not everyone was willing to admit that something was happening to us. Some passengers tried to ignore the situation and said we should just go on as if nothing were wrong. They had even organized a bridge tournament, an exhibition of artwork made from seaweed and shells – nothing original, however – a guessing game in which a wrong answer meant having to shed an article of clothing, and a super bingo tournament.)

'. . . is no reason to . . .'

(The whispering continued. If there was a reason and someone knew what it was, it would have to be stated. Shouts of *hurrah* could be heard, but they were unwarranted, as will be evident, and there were other cries that crashed against the side of the ship which, incidentally, was taking on water.)

'There is no reason to give up hope.'

(There followed a moment of silence, respected even by the actress.)

'It's true, we are traveling on a ship without a course.'

(A lot of people didn't approve of this type of frank language, it was something no one expected of a politician, a captain, or anyone in a position of authority.)

65

'But we must not be discouraged.'

(This was a little better. Why should we be discouraged?)

'Not at all. No! I say we shouldn't!'

(It takes courage to say no to something in public. Or, for that matter, to say yes.)

That someone would say no seemed to comfort a lot of people.

'No!'

(Some faint nos could be heard among those assembled.)

The waves, which were very close to us, began to break more gently.

The man shouted, this time a little louder, 'Who would benefit if we lose hope?' (The question seemed to have hit its mark. No one wants anyone else to reap the benefits of what is theirs, even if what they're reaping is a tragedy. Tragedies and everything they entail belong to the party concerned.)

'I think they want us to lose hope.'

Just in case it was true, a lot of people looked behind them, as if invisible beings were there waiting for our demise. This encouraged the others to believe that if some people had turned their heads, there must in fact be people lurking behind our backs, waiting to benefit. And the fact of knowing we weren't alone, that they were watching us, made us feel less lonely and more cautious.

It was determined by common, if unspoken, agreement that they were behind us, near the figurehead at the prow; from that moment onward, that part of the boat was considered a sort of contaminated area. Out of self-respect, as a matter of amour-propre and honor, no one dared to approach that area, although we would frequently cast contemptuous, hateful glares in that direction.

'Yes, they want us to lose hope,' the man insisted excitedly. 'So what should we do?'

66

The question, like any question, had quite an impact. People looked at one another and repeated it out loud or with their eyes. No one knew who was supposed to answer, so each person passed on the question to the person next to him or her.

'What are we supposed to do?' they said to one another. More than a question, it seemed like a statement.

'What are we supposed to do?' said the lion tamer to the doctor.

'What are we supposed to do?' said the bank clerk to the actress.

'What are we supposed to do?' the nurse repeated to a trapeze artist.

'Not lose hope,' said the speaker, his eyes fiery.

His clever answer was likewise repeated in unison. 'Not lose hope! Not lose hope!' we said to one another. Someone heard one wave repeat the words to another. We had the support of the sea – our strongest ally.

No one was going to lose hope, but if that were to happen, say by mistake, no one was going to admit to it. That way, they wouldn't benefit. This led us to undertake a number of activities that, until then – before knowing that we shouldn't lose hope – had been overlooked. Some passengers volunteered to scrub the deck, others, working as a team, divvied up the provisions and the water; our goal was organization. This seemed to be to the liking of the speaker, who was happily watching how those around him were carrying out the duties necessary for preserving the appearance of order. The actress said she would liven up the long nights spent out on the deck with free performances of her playing her favorite roles. To the delight of the passengers, the acrobats set up a little tent and began doing stunts. The doctor treated someone's stubborn cold.

The speaker felt the moment had come to take the floor again.

'Gentlemen,' he said, apparently addressing the ladies as well, 'gentlemen, we have grown accustomed to repetition, and surely, if repetition were to disappear, we would miss it. The time has come to . . .'

Unaccustomed to the metaphors of an age of uncertainty, some passengers anxiously glanced at their watches. It was exactly midnight. From our brief experience as members of the crew, we knew that that moment coincided with widespread apprehension. Although it was always possible to turn their heads and glare hatefully at the contaminated part of the boat near the figurehead, some passengers were feeling depressed and anxious. As our speaker told us, it was probably a result of the dark presence of the sea, of the repetitious lapping of the waves, of mariner's neurosis – a condition often suffered by sailors.

'It's time we made an organizational chart.'

No one had thought of that, but to a lot of people it seemed like a great idea. The good thing about it was that the chart wouldn't take up much space or get in the way of the leaps and tricks of the acrobats, and it would keep us busy. We spent a lot of time making up different versions. The position of captain naturally went to the speaker; there was no question about that. But the auxiliary ranks ushered in a lot of debate. We spent five days dealing with the issue of the chart. Meanwhile, we were running short of food, the boat began to list dangerously, and some passengers thought they'd seen a school of sharks closing in on us.

When the organizational chart was approved with near unanimity, morale improved considerably. Another of the captain's initiatives also helped: he suggested that the musicians play our favorite songs. We all knew there was a band on board but, because we were worried about our fate, it hadn't occurred to us to demand that they play. But after all, they were traveling for free with the express purpose of making the passengers happy.

The speaker ordered them to put on uniforms. I don't know if that was his own idea or if in the back of his mind he was remembering the sinking of the *Titanic*. In any case, they didn't have a choice in the matter.

We prepared ourselves, as if for a ceremony. We put on our best clothes. A team of volunteers hung garlands from the masts and waved flags. The flags all matched because they were made from a skirt donated, in an unexpected act of generosity, by the actress.

Bands always make me feel sad, maybe because they remind me of the regiment where I grew up that on blistering hot Sunday mornings would play the national anthem and – literally – execute a Beethoven passacaglia in the town park. Their uniforms were threadbare and their instruments dented and out of tune, but no one seemed to mind. Forced to always listen to the same thing, people had gotten used to it. This time something similar occurred. Whether it was because we were afraid of what lay in store for us (we hadn't lost hope, however – that was not allowed) or because the instruments had gotten wet (have I mentioned that the ship without a course was listing at times?), the songs we heard that night – 'Tea for Two,' 'Domino,' and 'As the Years Go By' – didn't sound right. It's true that that night, under the feeble light of the ship's lamps, the obese violinist did all he could to hold back the tears as he gripped his bow, that the trumpet player made every effort to make his notes scare away the outlines of nearby sharks, and that the passengers danced tirelessly, like windup dolls. The couples even changed partners in an effort to bring about a spirit of camaraderie, as if we were attending a garden party at a fancy house. Someone tried to allay

69

our fears about the water spewing out of the cabins, saying it was just like a fountain in a Moorish patio. No one stopped dancing when a high, but not especially loud, wave swept the first couple into the sea. They went without a scream. The space they freed up was quickly occupied by another couple. When the lights suddenly went out, the clown suggested a game of blind man's bluff. We immediately accepted. The clown offered to oversee the game himself, and we didn't even notice when he fell into the water. The sound of the ocean roaring in the darkness beckoned us. Realizing the danger we faced, the captain hurriedly climbed onto the platform.

'Dance! Everyone dance!' he shouted excitedly, and people did what they were told, as if under a spell. (Only once in my life have I observed a similar phenomenon: it was when Louis Armstrong was playing 'Sweet Lorraine.')

A big crash of water swept away several dancers. The band's vocalist was singing 'Sometimes I Love You.' The violinist introduced some interesting variations, and this time I have to say he got it right. It was too bad there was no piano on board; I would have accompanied him. Some of the notes were so beautiful they seemed to cut through the water. We were thinking that if they were still watching us, they could take a beautiful picture (using a flash, it was dark) and record the moment: the vocalist singing into the storm, 'If you go to Chicago, 66th Street . . . ,' the couples dancing, the captain up on the platform, just before the boat listed violently for the last time.

Letters

I receive a lot of letters and regret being unable to answer most of them, but I don't have a permanent address or a typewriter (writing longhand is increasingly unpopular). In any case, a lot of the letters don't reach me or they get lost somewhere along the way, but I'm sure that if the mailman knew me he would deliver them. It's all right with me if someone else receives the letters meant for me or if someone is reading them on my behalf. It's enough that a lot of people write to me, without even knowing where I am.

I'm not trying to change the established order of things or the way public administration works (I'm sure it takes a lot of effort to maintain order, and it's enough that public administration works at all, if only for a few people). And I wasn't trying to cause trouble when I asked a mailman I saw in the street if he had any letters for me. Since I don't have a permanent address, I couldn't tell if he was the mailman for my district. Very politely, I explained this to him when he asked which district I lived in. By the same token (although I don't know the rules on this), I don't believe that letters meant for me should remain undelivered just because they lack an address or a postal code. Unless, that is, you believe – and maybe the mailman, out of habit, did – that settling down in a house is a precondition for receiving letters. A lonely man can perfectly well send a message in a bottle that is picked up thirty years later at sea. (I read about this once in the newspaper. It happened during the Second World War. A serviceman on a boat out on the high seas wrote a message to his wife and stuffed it in a bottle that he tossed into the water. Thirty years later, a sailor picked it up near an island in the Pacific and took the trouble of mailing it to the addressee. The message, with its love code in a bottle like a butterfly in a glass case, had been floating around the oceans. Indelible and lost, a fish off course. The article gave no further information.)

'No one writes letters if they don't know where they're sending them,' he told me foolishly. I pointed out his mistake: in reality, the greatest letters ever written were never sent, even when the addressee had a fixed abode or a private mailbox. But in questioning him, I wasn't referring to the greatest letters but to the ones people write me, stick in an envelope, and post.

'You can file your complaint at the central office,' the mailman told me gruffly. 'Tell them where and when the letters were sent and who mailed them to you.'

I told him I had no idea who had written them or where they were coming from, since I'd never received them. Only after a mailman had delivered them to me could I know what letters we were talking about, and in that case I would have no reason to file a complaint or to state who had sent them or from where. And it didn't seem fair for the authorities to refuse to look for my letters just because I didn't know who had sent them.

'If you don't know who sent them or where they were sent from, the letters don't exist,' the civil servant replied categorically.

It seemed completely unfair that someone could say my letters didn't exist just because I hadn't received them yet, especially given my desire to read them and my perseverance in looking for them. 'So what do you do with letters that don't exist?' I asked the man.

'It depends,' he told me hesitantly. 'If the sender has put his address on the letter, like he's supposed to, the letter is returned to him. Otherwise, there's a waiting period.'

It seemed strange to me that a letter that didn't exist would be returned to its place of origin, and not, as you would expect, to the addressee. Especially if you consider that whoever sent the letter sent it to a person, not to a place, the indirect object being fundamental and the residence holding only transitive significance. We can imagine a letter being written to a traveler, to a man who moves through space and time, but no one thinks to write a letter to a house; the walls may have ears, but not eyes. As for the letters that don't exist but that are subject to a waiting period, what's the point of that period? What are letters that don't exist waiting for?

'It's standard procedure. If no one comes to claim them within six months,' the man said reluctantly, 'and if the address of the sender is unknown, they're filed in the basement of the central office.'

'How can I know when to go and claim a letter?' I asked humbly. (In dealing with authorities, deference is always a good idea.)

'You *shouldn't* go and claim them,' the mailman told me, as if I'd missed the most important point of his lecture. 'They're there to be stored. We know what country they come from, in what district they were posted, at what time they were sealed, and we know the name of the addressee, even though he may no longer live in the same place or the address is wrong or made up. So we classify them according to the place they were sent from and the date they were postmarked. We arrange them according to the city, the month, week, day, and time. Once the waiting period stipulated in the regulations has passed (which in no instance is to exceed six months), we take them down to the basement where they undergo further classification. I can't comment on that step because it's confidential. The supervisor and the archivist are the only ones who know about that. As you can imagine, that step is top secret. Once in the storage rooms, a letter is never lost.'

I receive a lot of letters and regret being unable to answer most of them, but I don't have a permanent address or a typewriter. In any case, a lot of the letters don't reach me, but I know there are people who write them and it's always possible to read them on the wings of birds, inside a bottle, or in the moist sands of the sea.

Flags

One flag is issued for each dead man. The simple ceremony is always performed in the same way and in the privacy of the home, without nosy onlookers. First, two officials arrive to convey the sad news to the relatives. Preparations for the delivery of the flag then begin. It should be pointed out that the presence of the officials has a moderating effect on the pain displayed by the families, who, out of a sense of decorum, restrain their expressions of grief. It's something about the uniforms and the measured expressions established by protocol that puts a limit on feelings of despair and that makes people cry in a more restrained manner.

For unrolling the flag, flat surfaces, such as livingroom tables, are favored. In complete silence (save for the subdued sobs of the women) and with an air of solemnity, one of the officials proceeds to carefully unfold the flag, mindful not to wrinkle it. The flag is unrolled across the table, like an altar cloth. Once the flag is fully extended, the other official addresses a few sober, restrained words to those assembled. He speaks of bravery, honor, and service to the homeland. When he has finished, there is a moment of silence. Then the same official folds up the flag. This is probably the most moving part of the ceremony, and many families are unable to refrain from crying. The flag is folded as follows: first, one of the corners is doubled over, forming a small triangle. Then that triangle is folded over itself and so on until the entire flag has been done. When the flag, by virtue of the geometric result of combining two equilateral triangles, is made into a square, one of the officials (not the one who folded it) proceeds to place it in the hands of a family member, who is greatly moved to receive it. The ceremony has then concluded, and the officials give the obligatory salute and depart.

Even though the flag doesn't weigh much when folded in that way, people are warned that it is somewhat unwieldy. Generally, the family member who received it doesn't know what to do with it. Placed under the arm, just below the right or left armpit, the flag allows one to move one's limbs freely but makes one very hot, especially in summer. Holding it in one's hands obstructs other necessary tasks, such as gesticulating. It is likewise difficult to find a place for it in the house. It would be disrespectful to hang the flag as decoration on a livingroom wall where it might clash with other household items, since the flag, in a certain way, is the dead father or son. The problem with using it as a sheet is that it is not exactly the same size as normal beds and allows the cold to creep in from the sides. Likewise, no one would feel comfortable eating on top of colors that represent the noble dead soldier. Some mothers place the flag on top of the vanity, but it gets dusty there and attracts moths. Apparently, the best place to store it is inside a nylon bag in a drawer full of old clothing. Even so, men can sometimes be seen in the streets with their flag rolled up under one arm, like the evening paper.

The use of flags is increasing and has made for a burgeoning industry. A lot of previously unemployed women now work zealously at making these national pennons to meet the needs of the army, the airforce, the navy, the infantry divisions, the airborne divisions, the special brigades, the flamethrowers, the expeditionary forces, and the highly selective combat aircraft crews. The country's population can be divided into two general categories: those who make flags and those who will receive flags. But these aren't entirely discrete categories. Often, a woman will be at her machine assembling the three different colored strips of fabric that make up our flag when she is interrupted by two officials carrying out the painful duty of issuing her a flag she didn't sew.

Since no two flags are exactly alike (variation can be found in the thickness of the threads, the distance between one band of color and another, the size of the stitches, and the way the edges are hemmed), a curious new hobby has emerged: collecting rare flags. Families study those that are in some way odd and reject those that were mass produced. A small black market for flags has sprung up on the fringes of the official one. But that unscrupulous traffic does not involve most of the country's families, who continue to carefully produce flags. All of this speaks well for the quality of contemporary patriotism.

The Avenues of Language

He would never just say, 'I ascended' or 'I descended.' He would say, 'I ascended up' or 'I descended down.' This linguistic oddity of his struck me as revealing: there's nothing innocent about syntax. Finding *ascend* unsettling, he probably wanted to reinforce the idea of the verb: *ascend* reveals the infinity of space – which is full of mystery and unknown dangers. As for *descend* (on its own, unaccompanied by a preposition), this verb is equally upsetting: it's never clear when the descent will come to an end or to what depths we will be led. The need to say 'descend down' emerges from this terror: we place a limit on the action of going down, we stop it at a specific point. Can you imagine descending forever, endlessly? It would be as unnerving as ascending forever. In any case, I seem to have discovered a certain difference between *up* and *down*. *Ascend up* reinforces the direction of the verb, since, strictly speaking, one can only ascend in that direction; now, it is possible that there is an imaginary place we call *up*, a specific place we ascend to. A mere leaf blown by the wind is incapable of ascending *up* in the way we ascend. We nearly always ascend a lot. We ascend buildings, skyscrapers, planes, mountains; we've even gone up to the moon.

One day the same individual told me, 'I was ascending up and didn't find you.' This sentence gave me considerable cause for reflection. As it happened, I had a small studio in the upstairs of a building. A dreary room painted gray by some previous tenant, it was full of old furniture and made me depressed, so I would stay there only for short periods of time. My initial confusion was attributable to the fact that he had employed the past continuous. Why hadn't he simply said, 'I ascended up and didn't find you.' He clearly wanted to make me suffer. In saying, 'I was ascending up and didn't find you,' he was prolonging the action of ascending and of not finding me. I continued to not be in my studio, he continued ascending and finding the room empty; my absence (not being there) was an ongoing absence. Had he said, 'I ascended up and didn't find you,' the action would have taken place in the past and I would have had no reason to feel guilty. Instead, the action lingered on; it was as if he were still going up and I had yet to arrive, would never arrive. I imagined him going up time and again. On some of his trips, the elevator wouldn't go down all the way. On reaching the second floor, it would go up again. Other times, he would go up and down without stopping, but no matter what he did he wouldn't find me. The elevator would creak, the door would rattle open, he would ring my studio doorbell, no one would answer, so he would retrace his steps, go down, but before reaching the lobby he would head back up to my studio, and I wouldn't be there. It seemed like it would be impossible to stop thinking about this, that the situation would just go on and on indefinitely unless he recast the sentence. In my mind, as we were drinking coffee at the corner café where the pinball machine chimed, its lights flickering in the mirror with a beer logo embossed on it, I was going to have to continue ascending and descending – even though steam was rising from our cups, we were smoking cigarettes, and the vapor was fogging the windows

79

(it's winter and it's cold outside.) Since I had yet to arrive at the studio and he was still going up, he could blame me for my absence from the studio while we were both at the café. To calm my nerves, I thought about how it would have been even worse had he said something like 'I have ascended up and I haven't found you' because that would have meant that I was likewise absent from the café with its gray marble tiles, gilt-framed mirror, fake palm trees, and fine porcelain cups. With that sentence, he would have made me disappear from the place. All of me taken together would not have been enough to make up for my absence. I don't know that he avoided that construction to spare me pain – a distressing feeling of unreality – but I silently thanked him all the same.

'I wasn't in my studio; I went up and then, almost immediately, came down,' I stated with considerable precision. 'I didn't feel like working. I went for a stroll in the street. But I didn't feel like walking either. I was sort of sleepy, feeling that kind of distance that protects one from anxiety.' My sentence established some order: the actions undertaken had been completed. I had gone up once, gone down once, walked aimlessly through the streets, and then entered the café and looked for a free table. I had sat down and lit a cigarette. Then he arrived.

'I got a little worried when I didn't find you,' he said, accepting the linguistic truce. 'I stayed in the lobby, smoking. Then I went outside. I thought you might be taking a walk.'

I was walking. I felt at ease with language. I was walking. I was wandering aimlessly down the avenues that were gradually becoming lighted. And even if I thought that walking always leads somewhere, my steps only led me inside words, where I feel safe.

Instructions for Getting out of Bed

If I make up my mind to get out of bed, I have to be very careful. No dogs or children can be loose, and the furniture has to be arranged. Because getting out of bed is a dangerous proposition. The area has to be clear – the lamps, wardrobes, tables, and all those handy things people put in houses to avoid emptiness need to be removed. That's why I give a lot of warning. I'll say something like, 'Tomorrow I'm going to get out of bed at five past nine. Check your watches, secure the furniture, fasten your seatbelts.' I always add five minutes to the hour because no one is punctual without a five-minute grace period.

Before leaving bed, I get myself ready. The day before I take care of all of those little details that are vital to a successful descent. The first thing I do is have a sign hung on the door so people won't disturb me. The sign states the precise date and time I plan to get out of bed and requests that no one disturb me because my plans can't be upset. Getting out of bed requires concentration. But to avoid accidents, I also have to be relaxed.

Before getting up, I study the whole room carefully, trying to memorize the location of everything I'll encounter. For example, on one of the walls, there's a window. I tried to cover it up several times, but I wasn't allowed to because, as I discovered, that would have been against local code. I'm very respectful when it comes to rules concerning peaceful coexistence; otherwise, there would be a lot more dangers out there than the ones that already exist. So in getting out of bed I have to take the window into account. It's not just any window: it's a window located near the top of the wall, in the part that slopes toward the ceiling. It lets in precisely the amount of light I can tolerate, not too much, not too little. People are very careless with light (and with everything else): they either use too much of it (maybe because they fear the ambiguity of shadows) or else (terrified that light makes it easy to see all those contours they hate) they live in semidarkness. Then in the summer they lie down anywhere (on dirty sand, in scraggly parks, next to polluted oceans) and let the sun burn their bodies, blistering and dehydrating the exposed skin (from a distance, they look like a company of crabs, a bunch of contorted limbs moving pell-mell). The window has to be closed when I get out of bed because a draft would pose a serious danger to my health. I use a map to study the location of different objects in the room. That way, I can plan my movements down to the last detail and avoid unpleasant surprises. For example, there's a wardrobe – the usefulness of which I won't comment on now – with a mirror on the door. Failing to avoid the mirror means I could be improperly reflected, shown someone I don't recognize myself in. So in crossing the room I have to be careful to avoid it. The carpet represents another problem. Although it offers some protection from the cold floor, it has the perverse habit of getting bunched up, so I have to move carefully to avoid tripping. (Another concern is that ants or other little insects might make nests in the folds or try to climb up my shoes: we know so little when it comes to the desires of animals.) Electrical outlets are another hazard. As is common knowledge, accidentally sticking your finger in one can result in a potentially lethal shock. And for some inexplicable reason, outlets are put on walls, at about the level of your hands – with no protective covering whatsoever.

Even when I've taken every conceivable precaution, there's nothing simple about getting out of bed. Sometimes I'm suddenly overcome with apprehension. I'm afraid of getting out of bed, of leaving the protection of the sheets, of no longer being lying down or sitting up. So I resist getting out. I know that on the floor I'll have to stand up, greet people, talk about this or that.

If I've announced when I'm going to get out of bed and then the time comes and I don't feel up to it, it's a lot worse: my mother, my sister, my uncle, or a friend will come over and ask me what's wrong. They'll choose their words carefully and try to encourage me – which in itself is terrifying. Having someone try to understand my fears only reinforces them, because it proves they're real, that the dangers exist. For instance, if someone says, 'Honey, you can get out now, I've moved all the furniture out of the way,' I panic, thinking I could have actually tripped on something (and I can never be sure they've gotten everything, every last thing, out of the way). If my sister comes over to the bed and tells me in a very caring voice, 'I'll help you get out. We'll do it slowly, very slowly,' I recoil, turn back, hide under the covers. There's a certain arrogance, a terrifying attitude of superiority, in the gentle way she offers to help. The apparent ease with which other people have resolved the problem of getting out of bed (something they do every day, as if it were the most natural thing in the world) doesn't make me respect or envy them. Since time immemorial, human beings have committed terrible acts with complete nonchalance (nonchalance is inimical to ethical judgment). Their example doesn't help. Anyway, a man never trips over the same stone twice; the second time around, neither the man nor the stone are the same. So it doesn't help to have my mother remind me, 'Darling, you can come out now, don't you remember the last time? You were afraid then, but nothing bad happened.' Of course not: once is enough. You can be ill a lot of times, but a single illness can kill you.

When I manage to get out of bed, the first thing I feel is happiness. I'm proud of what I've achieved. I feel like I've really excelled. On those occasions, I like to have people around to celebrate with (but not a lot of people: having a crowd in the room would completely disrupt the careful planning I've done). It's all right if they clap and cheer from a distance while I cautiously put one foot, then the other, onto the floor. But the happiness quickly fades.

On the ground, life is very difficult. For one thing, with everyone standing up, people feel they're indistinguishable from one another, which leads to hostility and competition. If I'm in bed, though, no one pays attention to me: people talk to each other as if I were just another object in the room, a lamp or a wardrobe. They make decisions and act without taking me into account, which spares me their aggressiveness and hostility. I don't affect things one way or another. If, on the other hand, I'm standing up (an uncomfortable position I never get myself into for long), I notice the way they look at me (not always fondly, to tell the truth), and I hear their quarrels, the turmoil of the house and all its disturbing echoes.

When I get out of bed I can't help but glance at the bit of street visible through the livingroom window. I see the cars racing by, their signal lights flashing as they go off somewhere. They stop very obediently at red lights and then, all at the same time, set off, taking possession of the street. (In my nightmares, the enormous traffic light gives the go-ahead and the mysterious, metallic cars, with their powerful shiny jaws and no one behind the wheel, charge ahead, powered by remote control.) The people who drive the cars feel very powerful. I prefer the pedestrians, but I don't understand where they're going, why they cross the street without stopping, without greeting one another, as if they were ants or dolphins. I've also seen people in uniform – doormen, guards, elevator attendants, employees of one kind or another. Wearing their suits, they all take their roles very seriously, never making a mistake, as if it all came to them naturally. I've asked my mother if people don't sometimes hesitate in elevators before pressing a button, if they always know exactly which one they're going to push, if there isn't a moment when they can't make up their minds. She told me it doesn't happen, or if it does it's because the person has bad eyesight. For example, bus drivers. They never stray from their route. They repeat their movements exactly, without any variation. They don't suddenly head for a park or drive to the waterfront because they want to have a look at the sea. I'm also surprised by the crane operator who repeats the same, parsimonious movements (clumps of black earth rising gradually, like guilt you can't get rid of); he raises the huge iron shovel and then slowly lowers and buries it into the pile of debris; then he fills it up, lifts it, and finally dumps the load in the truck, never feeling the urge to play, to draw circles in the air, to pick up something he shouldn't.

The whole spectacle of the street disturbs and terrifies me, which is why I immediately stop looking.

So my stays on the floor are brief. Even though my doctor says it's beneficial for me to be out of bed, that it's good for my muscles and my circulation, I know it isn't good for my soul. Frazzled and nervous, I go straight back. I hide there, under the sheets, covered and protected. For a while, no one thinks about me, except when it's mealtime or a question of personal hygiene, and even then they treat me like a broken doll, a machine that's out of order. A busted mannequin. Otherwise, regardless of whether I'm lying down or standing up, the world doesn't seem to notice my participation in it, despite desperate gestures intended to show the contrary. The world will always be a distant place.

Airports

I

Despite what their name might suggest, they aren't flying ports; they're the roosts of birds and of men. Sometimes a plane makes a mistake while landing and a catastrophe occurs. Like when on foggy days a half-blind pigeon lands on the sidewalk and collides with another one that, in turn, makes a fuss; and for a while there's commotion among the pigeons.

The most important thing in an airport is for the floor to be waxed and polished so that children can slide from one end to the other (which they call cities). That way, well before getting on the plane, they've already made the trip.

Some adults regularly dream about airports. They love that feeling of worldliness they get in them, the lulling sound of flights being announced, being rocked by the wings of a plane that transports them almost imperceptibly. Other people love airports because they enjoy feeling suspended between one city and another, between one time zone and another, that ongoing sensation of having neither left nor arrived; something tells them that they are inside and outside at the same time, at the center and at the margin. Some of those who stay behind dream of escaping.

The passengers departing for Amsterdam experience a sensation of nostalgia, and the voice of the stewardess calling passengers for Tripoli is smooth and glides like a very prim little girl down a corridor.

Others love those moments of premonition in airports when suspicions are suddenly confirmed (about the length of a flight) and how, through the confusing fog of the little window, a distant light can resemble the future.

Those who stay behind tend to experience a sensation of emptiness, those who go away of frustration. That's when both the traveler and the person who stays at home look at the airport and realize that it is an island.

II

Other people, people who love danger, like airports because they know that in them one is always about to lose or miss something.

Some people arrive at the last minute, forgetting promises and suitcases; they appear light and airy, as if upon boarding the plane they could leave behind the past as easily as an old overcoat. Then the stewardess announces, 'Fasten your seatbelts securely,' and the man finally sighs and restrains what he was about to lose.

Other people arrive at the airport with a lot of time to spare: half asleep, as if under the influence of a mild sedative, they take to the airport as if it were their mother's womb. They stretch their legs, yawn, smile innocently, slowly smoke their cigarettes, read magazines, look out the windows. None of this is to say that they board the plane on time: the wait is so pleasant that often, feeling drowsy, they decide to remain on the airport bench, lulled by the maternal voices of stewardesses who monotonously announce numbers and names.

Those who travel least are doubtless flies: they're afraid of heights. On a flight from Montreal to New York, however, I came across one. It was fat and confused, like those female passengers who arrive late and are afraid they're at the wrong gate. It finally landed on my neighbor's bald spot. We couldn't open the window to let it out, even though it was very dizzy – we'd never committed a crime at that altitude. We were gliding along up at twenty-nine thousand feet. I don't know whether the fly was feeling more vertigo or if I was.

III

At the Toronto airport an unusual conference was held – for travelers who have never managed to depart. Invitations were sent out by mail and a satellite network was used to simultaneously broadcast the sessions at different airports. Travelers arrived by car or train from their respective parts of the country. Toronto was the clearinghouse for information and the site where discussions were held. From the comfort of leather chairs that would never fly, participants from various parts of the world told their stories. There were silver ashtrays, almond bags, coasters with the names of different international airports on them, duty-free cigarettes, imported liqueurs, and, on the table, an exquisite silver tower with a plane that flew circles around it and would quiver with the slightest change in atmospheric pressure.

For one reason or another, none of the participants had ever been able to leave the airport. Initially discouraged for perfectly understandable reasons, they had finally given up on their trips, once their excuses became less plausible. Although the number of travelers unable to depart from one particular airport (which will remain unnamed) might raise suspicions that there are people blocking the movements of travelers, the consensus was that these were random, unorchestrated events. A man who had tried unsuccessfully to depart from the Copenhagen airport twenty-five times was named Honorary President. Honorary mentions were given to stationary passengers at the London, Ezeiza, and Santiago airports. But the most popular figure was the would-be traveler from New York who rented a lounge at JFK where he could conduct his business affairs, receive visitors, and enjoy his leisure time.

At first, he returned home every evening to his white-trimmed house located just past the wrought-iron bridge over the Hudson. But traffic jams, unforeseeable accidents, and fatigue convinced him that it would be preferable to not only work at the airport but also to sleep there. He didn't need a television set because airport lounges are full of them; the heat was free; the showers were excellent; and he never had to go far to find someone to talk with. By sleeping in the rented airport lounge, he even saved on taxes. He could always meet with busy clients who were on their way somewhere, and he avoided long, lonesome nights of insomnia in bed with his wife. All he had to do was take a few steps and he was right in front of the huge window where he could see the planes arriving day and night. It was stimulating, exciting. He could always exchange a few words with arriving passengers – about the weather, inflation, politics in other countries, floods, epidemics, movie premieres. Another advantage of living in the airport is that cigarettes are always available because the shops never close: can you imagine the pleasure of buying a pack of Marlboros at four in the morning without leaving your bedroom? The airport had twenty-four-hour medical services, the restaurant food was just as bad as anywhere else, and most of the girls sliding down the polished corridors were pleasant and nice.

The conference lasted three days. When it was over, the participants returned to their respective homes by car, bus, or train. Many turned around for a last nostalgic look at the airport.

90

Time Heals All Wounds

I'm always in a hurry, it's a matter of temperament. When I broke up with her I went straight to a pawn shop. I needed a lot of time to put on my wounds, so they would stop bleeding and heal quickly. The wounds, some deeper than others, were in different places, and all of them hurt. I had a serious lesion to my pride that wouldn't stop bleeding, and I thought going out in public like that didn't look right. The wound to my plans for the future was infected: the sepsis was creeping into my Sunday afternoons and contaminating my dreams at night, provoking insomnia.

'I need a large supply of time,' I told the solicitous man behind the counter. 'Put it on my wounds and I'll go right to bed. I want to wake up cured.'

The man looked at me indifferently. 'What kind of time do you want?' he said, expressionless. He had blond hair and pale, transparent eyes. He was wearing an old suit and had a long thumbnail, which might be good for scratching tables. His indifference showed that he was a man in the habit of buying and selling.

'It's all the same to me. I'll take any kind, so long as it heals,' I told him.

Rather disinterestedly, the man looked over at some shelves, which were crammed full of all kinds of things – household items, lamps, used clothing, memoirs, old typewriters, potted plastic flowers, empty fish tanks. 'You'll have to wait awhile,' he told me. 'I don't have any time in stock.'

I hate to wait. It seemed like a good idea, though. My wounds were exposed, bleeding. A good bandage might cure me. What kind of time did I need? Empty time, like my days since she's been gone? An indeterminate time? Ten, twelve, fifteen doses of time? I'd buy as many as necessary and put them on right away. I'm a man who loves speed, and my wounds were healing slowly.

Just then a girl opened the door. She was very well dressed, had short blond hair, and seemed distinctly frail. I was afraid that opening the door would make her fly away like a feather, that her feelings, ideas, and desires would explode in a thousand pieces. I would have had to bend over to pick up the pieces, which might have embarrassed her. She seemed somewhat jittery. As a matter of fact, I had the feeling she was always somewhat jittery.

'I'd like to sell a little time,' she said in a voice that was low but not timid. 'Right now,' she added. She must have really needed to get rid of it. She hadn't even waited for the man to reply.

'That's exactly what I'm looking for,' I said, before the salesman had a chance. 'I'll buy it, as much as you have. I'll pay whatever you want.'

She seemed a little surprised by my interjection.

'I don't think this time is very useful,' she said earnestly. 'It's very uncomfortable for me, I don't know what to do with it, it bothers me. I'd like to get rid of it in a bloodless, you know, honest way.'

'All of your time, ma'am?' I asked, a little surprised.

She was leaning over the counter, revealing a gorgeous shirt sleeve, which was embellished by a cufflink. The cufflink was a golden iris against a black background. I might have wanted to have those cufflinks and maybe even the woman who was wearing them, but at that very moment I felt a terrible cramp in my leg. I'd had it – I needed a cure.

Leaning gently against the counter in her mauve blouse, she seemed to be mulling over how much time she was willing to sell me.

'I don't know how much to keep for myself,' she admitted a bit nervously. 'The truth is, I like to kill it in different ways, throw it out the window, squander it, squish it between my hands, put it on the bed and take it apart: how time enslaves! It always comes back to haunt me. Take as much as you want, it doesn't do me any good. Anyway, whatever's left over will seem very long.'

I bought a bunch of time from her. She breathed happily, like a little girl just relieved of an unpleasant chore. She invited me for a cold drink (she wants to kill the rest of it, I thought to myself), but I wanted to get going right away: my wounds were still bleeding and they hurt a lot. I was going to soak them in time, for a long time, for an empty time, like the time I'd just bought, in time that was superfluous and unimportant but that would nevertheless heal my wounds.

Love Story

She said she loved me and offered me her life.

Initially, I was touched – it was the first time that had ever happened to me. But after a while my shoulders started hurting: there's no such thing as a light, easily wielded life. Being submissive and obedient, I put the heavy load on my back and headed straight for the mountain. Her life was awkwardly balanced, and sometimes it would rub against my shoulder blades, which made my skin begin to chafe, turn red, and wear thin. When one side hurt a lot, I would arch my back and try to shift the weight to the other side.

Before I had completed the first part of the journey I noticed that one of my ribs had shifted and was digging into my stomach. I got worried and wanted to get rid of the burden, which solemnly swore she loved me and settled down more comfortably on my shoulders.

With my rib digging into my stomach, it was hard to eat or move, but I discovered a new way of breathing – in two steps, the first slow and shallow, the second deeper. This allowed me to continue walking. I noticed that as I was walking a lot of people would stop to congratulate me. Word of her love had spread and I became vaguely famous. My feet were bleeding and I gave up wearing shoes. I wished that like one of those huge sea turtles I had a thousand-year-old shell to protect my back.

94

Under the weight of her life, I began to walk with a stoop. I couldn't see the sky or the tops of trees, birds flying through the air, or the butterflies flittering on stormy days. Although sometimes I really missed the clouds and rainbows, I got used to slouching and to seeing only what was on the ground.

In the beginning, when I would stop at the bank of a pristine river to have a drink or to rest for a while, she would let me put her life on the ground (I would watch her carefully while eating or drinking so she wouldn't get lost or be carried off by a stranger). That way I could rest a little. But one day, when we'd been walking for a while, she announced her decision never to leave me. Under all that weight, I couldn't raise my head to look at her, but it was obvious how adamant she was about it. She said her decision was born of a deep love for me. Although my back was doubled over, my muscles were trembling, my feet were lacerated and my rebellious ribs were moving about, I had the privilege of her undivided love.

'She can't go on being stuck to me if I don't want her to be,' I thought to myself as I moved my shoulders to better accommodate the load. The mountain was near and at any moment I would begin the frightening ascent. 'No matter how much she protests,' I continued, 'I'll still be able to put her down for a moment to have a drink or to sleep, no matter how much she cries or nags or pretends to be sick: all I have to do is shake my shoulders and she'll fall off.' But I was wrong. When I tried to shake her off my back and put her on the ground for a moment, I discovered I couldn't. Her vital organs had been secreting a yellowish liquid, a viscous substance that dried and made her stick to me once and for all. With the determination of a castaway, I used my hands to try and break the hard crust that joined us. 'It's no use,' she told me from just above my kidneys. 'My love will last forever, it's unbreakable,

95

indestructible. It flows from my breasts and hardens as soon as it reaches you, the metal that sticks to your ribs comes from my womb. Now we'll never be apart,' she said triumphantly.

I shook in vain, trying to free myself of the burden. I only managed to get myself even more tired. Like a clumsy snail slowly plodding on under the weight of its shell, with each step I took I unwillingly carried her with me. I even thought to get close to the mountain and brutally smash my load against the hard, insomnious rocks. But I quickly realized that, like a raging beast, I would destroy myself at the same time.

So I began the ascent. The secretions from her organs, sticky liquids spilling onto my hands, came more frequently and numbed my fingers. Thick layers made one part of my body stick to another, which made it even harder for me to move. I felt her secretions flowing over my back, making the crust that joined us stronger and stronger.

At night I would be exhausted and sleep fitfully, wet from the liquids that flowed now and then from her armpits, pores, and legs. One morning I woke up and found my mouth was covered with a sticky yellow mesh that prevented me from speaking. While moving around in her sleep she had exhaled the sinewy strands that had hardened on my lips. I struggled to break the film, but it was impossible: I was ascending the mountain a mute.

It's a difficult ascent. My back is getting more stooped all the time. I no longer see other people on the trail; it's not just because we're in a remote, dangerous part of the mountain: if I were to cross paths with someone, I wouldn't even notice because I'm so hunched over under all this weight. In addition, my fame has died out and, being so skinny, with my bones exposed and all these shell-like scabs, I don't think anyone would recognize me.

I'm not concerned about making it to the end of the journey. The summit is still a long way off and I'll never reach it. Anyway, I'm old, or at least I look very old. I know I'll die soon and I've tried to warn her. I'm getting thinner all the time, there's no skin left on my feet, my bones are protruding. Since the shell makes it impossible for me to speak or eat, I warned her by gesticulating. She immediately comforted me. 'I love you,' she said. 'I offered you my life; how could you not give me yours?'

A Sense of Duty

In my dreams, I work hard. As soon as I finish one task, something else urgently demands my attention. I do a lot for humanity, in my dreams. People have the frivolous habit of ignoring danger, of exposing themselves to all sorts of hazards, so as each night goes by I have even more to do. I'm not just referring to my mother, who lives in a house with no doors that's buffeted by the wind and that I continually have to shore up with beams and posts, or to my little sister, who has the habit of walking perilously close to the brink of cliffs while wearing nothing but a transparent silk dress (it's really strange, but at the age of five she stopped growing; time passes but has no effect on her – her appearance doesn't change and we all think it's perfectly normal that she still looks the same); in my dreams I also have to protect a lot of people I don't even know but whose lives are in danger. Especially people at the beach. Confused by the sun, excited by being so close to the sea, distracted by innocent activities like playing with a ball, swimming, or running along the shore, they take no precautions whatsoever; in their mad relish they disregard the dangers all around them. Careless fathers sometimes set their children loose at the shore, women naïvely venture into the water, children search beneath the waves for stones. The sea is no mystery to me: behind its inoffensive façade, its gentle lapping against the rocks, lurks a despot. When

98

I arrive at the beach, I immediately recognize signs of danger. I sense a huge wave – a lonely, unrestrainable killer – welling up out on the horizon, on that narrow grayish-violet line just below the sky.

It's important to point out that what is overwhelming about my dreams is not the seriousness of my responsibilities but *consciousness*. I could do the same things – clear obstacles from the roads, shore up walls, mislead pursuers, evacuate burning homes – and do them with the same determination and sense of urgency; what is overwhelming is knowing that I am the only one who perceives these dangers, who is conscious of them and who sees them approaching, implacably. Like Cassandra who was cursed by a vengeful god and turned into a prophet heard by no one, in my dreams my mission is a solitary one. No one else has the same premonitions.

The unsuspecting bathers cheerfully venture down to the water's edge. Meanwhile, out at sea, an enormous wave is building up. It gathers silently at the bottom of a place we've never been. How I feel it slowly welling up. Born of other people's unawareness, it is in no hurry and takes its time. A tall column of water, a liquid mountain, it rises in solitude without spilling its contents and advances mercilessly. That's when I try to draw the sea curtain. At the shore (which, now that everyone is in the water, is empty and resplendently white), the thick, coarse fabric that is the surface of the sea ripples, like the skin of a giant pachyderm. The ocean is a huge tarp, a tent over an unseen circus. You can tug at its ends, from a thick twisted rope. When you pull, the sea becomes calm, taut like a flat, pleatless stage curtain. But the rope is heavy and burns. Leaning back with the weight of my body, I first tug in toward the shore. From somewhere, my father encourages me, tries to cheer me on. It's so exhausting (what with the bottom of the sea pulling with all its might) that I sometimes lose a little ground. Then the wave, as big as a monster, rises and opens its frothy mouth. But despite the burns on my hands and arms, I quickly try to recover the ground I've lost; I continue to concentrate on pulling. I have to pull the curtain until it reaches the pier and tie it to a bollard. When it's too much for me, I turn my back to the sea and run the thick rope over my shoulders so I can pull even harder. But turning away from the sea makes me nervous because it keeps me from seeing the wave I'm supposed to be watching over.

I pull with all my might, which is insignificant compared with the weight of the gray fabric of the sea, and I'm afraid my strength will give out at any moment. Then the catastrophe would strike. A moment comes when I can't go on pulling. I grow weak and tired and look on desperately as the rope I had held so tightly slips through my hands and the curtain gathers and rises, revealing an immense, hostile, vengeful sea.

It all happens with the speed of the worst catastrophes: with nothing to restrain the gigantic wave (it's horrifying to remember that I didn't have the strength to hold on to the rope), the liquid mountain advances, rushes toward the incautious swimmers who, surprised and frightened, sink to the infinite depths.

Between a Rock and a Hard Place

There's hardly any room between a rock and a hard place. If I try to get away from the rock and move back toward the hard place, I freeze. If I try to get away from the hard place and move forward, the rock presses against my head. Any accommodation I try to find between the two is false so I reject it. Both the rock and the hard place are determined to do me in, annihilate me, so I refuse to opt for one or the other. If the rock were softer than the hard place or the hard place less jagged than the rock, I could choose between them, but anyone who knows anything about either one will tell you the differences between a rock and a hard place are only superficial. I also know I can't postpone my death by trying to live in that miniscule space between them. Not only is the air thin, it's full of poisonous gases and particles. The rock inflicts small embarrassing bruises (which I try to cover up), and the hard place is so cold my lungs get congested, despite my feeble coughs. If I could manage to slip out from between them (an impossible feat), the rock and the hard place would have to face one another. But without me in between them, their strength would be so diminished the rock might crumble and the hard place might go soft. Still, there's no crack to escape through. If I move away from the rock, the hard place moves closer, and if I back away from the hard place, the wall closes in on me.

I've tried to distract the rock, even suggesting games we might play, but it's a very shrewd rock, and when its jagged edges aren't aimed at my head, they're aimed at my heart. As for the hard place, yes, I sometimes forget that it's icy cold, and when I'm exhausted I try to lean on it for support. But as soon as I do that, a deathly chill reminds me of the true nature of the hard place.

I've lived like this for the last few months. I don't know how much longer I can avoid being destroyed by one or the other. The space between the rock and the hard place is getting narrower all the time, and I'm running out of energy. I'm indifferent to my fate. Knowing that I'll either die of pneumonia or be crushed by the rock doesn't worry me. But I can say conclusively: between a rock and a hard place is no place to live.

The Effect of Light on Fish

I live alone, well, with my fish tank. It's a big rectangular tank with a neon light. Inside, the fish move about leisurely, absorbing air, swimming amid the algae and the lichen and above the little stones at the bottom.

It's set up in the living room, next to the bedroom. In addition to the neon light that's never turned off (I couldn't stand the idea of the fish moving around in the dark, in the loneliness of the house), the tank has an electronic oxygenation system that automatically refreshes the air.

My life has changed a lot since I bought the fish tank. Now I go straight home after work, anxious to sit down in front of the aquarium and watch their hypnotic movements, to drift along with them through water that's full of beards and filaments. I go to bed late, reluctant to pull myself away from the tank. Some of the fish hide behind seashells, as if they were trying to flee my gaze, to protect their intimacy. Fish aren't all the same. If you know how to observe them, get to know them, you recognize their peculiarities. Some of them have strange habits. Take the little black one. That fish never goes up to the surface. It likes to be in the middle and isn't curious about what's happening up above. *I don't know my next-door neighbor. I've never seen him.* The gold-colored one, on the other hand, is very timid and hides whenever I change the water.

103

I'm very careful when it comes to feeding the fish. As is well known, they have voracious appetites and can eat themselves to death if you give them too much food. So I bought a scale, and I'm meticulous about measuring how much I feed them. This doesn't rule out conflicts. Some fish take advantage of their greater size and, without thinking about the others, try to devour more than their share.

I buy the fish at a shop near where I live. *In modern apartment buildings, no one knows anyone else.* I like to discuss the habits of fish with the owner, but he doesn't know much about the subject. In addition to fish, he sells plants, dogs, and cats. He's told me that the popularity of fish tanks is on the rise and that the country's birthrate has declined. But I'm going to find another supplier: this guy sells them in plastic bags full of water, which makes me feel like I'm buying packaged fish. I may as well say, 'Half a kilo of red fish, please.' *In this city, you can die and no one will know the difference.* I have a special fascination with the fish tank. I put my chair in just the right place, in front of the tank (have I mentioned that it's rectangular?), turn off the lights, and sit down to watch the fish. I know it's impossible to think about nothing and that if you try to your spirit becomes more restless than normal. But I've managed to do just that, fixing my eyes on the fish tank. It's a form of hypnosis. The fish glide by perfectly calm on their way to nowhere in particular. The water barely moves, the plants are still. The silky moss radiates a metallic calm. The algae look like syrup. Sometimes they stick to my fingers when I'm cleaning the fish tank. If the phone rings, I don't answer, I don't want anyone to distract me from my observations.

There are little fish and bigger fish. I try not to show a preference for one kind or another. People may not know this, but fish are touchy. *I read in today's paper that the body of a woman was found in her house. She'd been dead for two months. The neighbors were tipped off by the smell in the stairwell. Until then, no one had noticed. Come to think of it, it's a good thing corpses smell.* But I confess, the iridescent ones are my favorites. They're small and nimble and have a phosphorescent streak across their fins (like the ones across stamps with the Queen of England on them). They flit around the tank like shooting stars. I wonder if the red fish has realized my preference for the iridescent ones. I know a woman who lives alone and who has her nephew give her a call every morning so that he can make sure she hasn't died. He's very responsible and calls her from the office every day. 'I haven't died yet,' she answers. She can't stand the idea of being found dead a long time after having passed away. Since buying the fish tank, I go out less often. I think it would be cruel to leave them alone. They're used to my gaze, I know they recognize me. Sometimes I used to accept invitations to go out. I would play pool, have a beer, or watch television on a color screen. Now I go straight home. Especially now that I know my fish tank offers excellent entertainment: I can watch the fish devour one another. This is more entertaining than theater or boxing, it's an exciting spectacle. Sometimes I get so wrapped up that I skip work. It's a slow, stubborn, merciless fight to the death.

There's always one fish that starts the chase, which can go on all day, sometimes for an entire week. When that happens, it's hard for me to concentrate at work. I'm afraid that when I get home, the pursuer will have devoured his victim and that I'll only find out when I count the fish.

At first, it might look like a game. But something about the terrified gaze of the fish that's fleeing makes you realize the struggle is real. The pursuer never rests and isn't discouraged by repeated setbacks. It hides and stalks its victim. The prey has no respite, no friendly algae or protective rocks, no peace. The pursuer appears from behind a shell and darts after its prey. The only way the prey can save itself is by flitting its tail fins more skillfully or forcing itself to swim faster. Even if it goes up to the surface, the pursuer is right behind it, and if it descends, the pursuer is still on its trail. Sometimes the pursuer manages to press its mouth against the side of the fish that's fleeing but doesn't wound it. I've watched some very long pursuits.

Even after the pursuer finally bites the victim's tail, the agony can drag on for a long time. That's when you can witness a very interesting phenomenon: the other fish that until then had been indifferent to the chase and refrained from siding with one party or the other get actively involved in the hunt, trying to bite the victim, to yank off some flesh. Even the smallest fish participate. The trail of blood the victim leaves behind attracts them and they all bare their teeth and try to corner the victim. It's exciting to see how the spectators participate in the spectacle.

Devouring a wounded fish is a slow and tricky operation. The other members of the tank come from all different directions, take a bite, and then retreat. Meanwhile, the wounded fish still tries to defend itself, hiding among the rocks, moss, or lichen. Conflicts, altercations, and clashes break out among the pursuers. Sometimes the fish that takes the last bite is bitten by the fish behind it.

When one of the pursuers is more ferocious and outdoes all the others, I separate it from the group for a while so that the rest of the fish can compete more fairly. Then I throw it back into the tank. Its return to the water incites fear, introduces a slight disturbance.

After discovering the fish fights, I stopped accepting visitors. I like to watch the spectacle alone without the distraction of unsolicited observations. Once, I invited two friends over to watch the fight but they got out of hand. They bet on one of the fish, got excited, spilled beer on the furniture, used rough language, and nearly smashed the fish tank. They didn't want to leave: they were ready to wait it out on my couch until one fish swallowed the other. 'Sometimes it takes days. Some fish just don't want to die,' I told them. They started pleading with me to let them stay until the end. Ever since then, I've refused to have visitors.

It's unfortunate but sometimes a really voracious fish manages to devour the others before it's time for me to go to bed. Then I go running off to the house of the guy who sells plants, dogs, cats, and fish tanks. I plead with him to sell me a half-dozen red fish and a half-dozen black fish.

'Are you sure?' he asks. 'I don't think they get along, I think they devour each other.'

'A half-dozen red ones, a half-dozen black ones,' I tell him nervously.

'You know, I used to be a bricklayer. I lost my job, but that was my trade.'

With my dozen new fish, I can go home happy. I put them in the tank right away. Then I sit down and wait. Sometimes it takes a day or two before they decide to fight. In the meantime, I feed them well, make sure their meals aren't too large or too small. I change their water and adjust the oxygen tube. And I never turn off the light.

Keeping Track of Time

I arrived in a city where the children all wanted to know what time it was. They seemed very serious as they made their way through the streets. Their hands in their pockets, self-absorbed, an air of busyness about them, they directed their eyes downward, at a reckoning of minutes and seconds that might have been lost.

The trees were barren and the sidewalks cold. One of the children came running toward me. The windowpanes were foggy. No sooner had he passed me than he turned around (a movement he might have thought to make all along but that caught me by surprise) and asked, 'What time is it?'

I withdrew the big silver watch I always carry in my pocket. It's heavy and in consulting it I have to go through the motions slowly, given the solemn task of verifying the passage of time. I lifted the cover (which is oval shaped and elegantly engraved on the sides), exposing its pearly face, just like when the velvet curtain at the theater is slowly drawn back and reveals the stage. (I have to use both hands to hold it, not only because of its considerable weight but also out of reverence.) 'It's five past six,' I answered, as the well-mannered boy got ready to resume his race.

On the other side of the street, a boy with blond hair and glasses (the frames of which seemed too big for his short, freckled nose) came running up. He was in a big hurry and concentrating hard on the act of hurrying. When he reached me he stopped and exclaimed, 'Excuse me. Can you tell me what time it is?'

Even though I already knew the answer, it seemed impolite not to take the big watch out of my pocket and verify the position of its hands: a hint of objectivity got mixed in with the apparently superfluous act of checking the time. I opened the cover (the boy was indifferent to the maneuver), and after looking sternly at the watch's hands I told him, 'Ten past six.'

He seemed neither satisfied nor dissatisfied, and quickly raced off.

My stroll had become strange, as if the yellow light of the somber dusk had me suspended from some unknown realm. It made me think of what argonauts lost at sea must feel, or space travelers in a never-ending orbit. A girl with cantaloupe-colored braids came to my side and didn't ask me anything. This gave me a certain feeling of relief and allowed me to gaze more calmly at the linden trees along the sidewalk. The empty street seemed to levitate, but the wintry landscape was familiar. I walked past a closed café (the window, which had no curtains, revealed lonely stacked chairs, burnt-out candles, and empty unshimmering glasses on the counter), then a laundromat whose gray machines (resembling the eyes of giant Cyclopes) were washing rhythmically, and a restaurant specializing in Italian food. Finally, I reached the corner. Three children running together, without one ever overtaking either of the other two, passed me. When the third of them was in front of me he suddenly stopped (like automatons, the other two immediately stopped as well). In a clear, expressionless voice, he said:

'Sir, can you tell me what time it is?'

It was six twenty. They immediately continued on their way, running in formation, one never overtaking another.

The sky had a purple hue (like on one of those winter afternoons), and they were hurrying off somewhere. I didn't know where they were going but it seemed to me that wherever that was, the minutes and seconds were important. Why that would be I didn't know, or else I had forgotten.

Statues, or, Being a Foreigner

I arrived at a large, empty town square whose gray paving stones seemed to have been laid only recently. There were no buildings or houses around it, just a few tufts of trees. It was its oblong shape that made me realize this was a town square. Some squares don't have a clock tower, wooden benches with iron dragon's feet, a little church, or even a simple jailhouse, so I recognize them by their shape. This was one of those squares. The trees were withering, their leaves dry and their trunks looking like they were about to crack. I wandered down one side of the square and observed the indistinct pattern of the leaves. But the square was full of statues. I couldn't tell if they had been there always, or only for a little while. They were in groups of three or four, in circles. Some were seated, knitting, and their bodies merged with the chairs, forming a single piece. Others had their mouths open, as if about to utter some sound or to begin speaking. Those furthest away were standing, leaning against the older statues. They had an expression of ennui, perhaps even of lassitude.

I looked at one of them, a young woman with a pale, listless body, her limp hair gathered in a bun at the back of her neck. She had a vacant gaze. I think she was looking beyond the square, beyond the tufts of withering trees. That most distant group formed a curve, an incomplete circle that left a small opening. They almost seemed to be moving, their skirts fluttering a circle, their arms away from their bodies, their heads bowed as if by the wind, a wind that only blew on that side of the square, in the small area they occupied (the landscape was otherwise motionless, still, calm). There were no outsiders, no foreign presence in any of the groups. Not even a dog could be seen roaming about on that frozen dawn. And yet, it seemed to me that the paving stones had been laid very recently. The statues didn't appear to have noticed, however. Self-absorbed in their circles, in their concentric movements, they did not appear to notice anything around them.

I felt like a foreigner, a disturbance, although the sort of disturbance I represented could only be perceived by me. Not wanting to intrude, I looked for a path that would lead me away from the gathering. No one was watching me, and it was precisely that inattention that made me feel out of place. It was then that I discovered that at the heart of being a foreigner is a void, not being recognized by those who occupy a place solely by virtue of their occupying it.

At the Hairdresser

They're seated in a row along one side of the salon, and anyone entering sees them only in profile, as happens with the figures in the Leonor Fini painting, *The Permanent Miters*. There's a sour smell about the place. Now and then you hear the buzz of some electronic hair-manipulation gadget. Calmly, in religious pose, the women await each stage of the ritual. Mother Superior (wearing her nuncio's gown) issues concise orders; she points at a basin, demands some dye. The bottles on the shelves are bathed in light.

An initiation tunic is placed over the most recent arrival, the ends tied around her neck with a ribbon. She is then ushered over to a chair reserved for her. She is ordered to lean back and place her hands in her lap as the ablution begins. Someone spreads incense around the salon. From their respective recesses in the wall, the plants – their stems rigid, as if made of plastic – preside sternly over every stage of the ritual. Then the unction: someone pours water into the basins, wets the tips of her fingers, and massages the foreheads and necks of the elect. Some ointment is applied to another woman (the second in the row of those seated against the wall), and strands of her hair are painstakingly separated from one another; then, when they are sticking out like crosses, they are clipped together and a needle is stuck through them. Someone else works her way down the row of sitting women and stops to tar the face of each one. She spreads the cream slowly, ceremoniously, aiming to cover the marks and stretch lines, to hide the underlying shapes. The row is gradually transformed into a succession of gravestones.

Mother superior steps back. She goes over by the wall in order to get a better look at her work. With hidden satisfaction, she admires the identical petrified masks. She calls for a dab of cement around a woman's eye, wipes off some extra lime from someone's neck. Then she steps back again to consider the adjustments. You can hear the distant buzz of a face-destroying firmer. The plants don't seem to notice the noise, the sunlight, or the moisture from the baptismal fonts.

The first one to leave deposits her oblation at the door: dark bills like a tapestry on the counter.

The others remain behind, silent, strapped to their chairs, as the leader of this ceremony raises above her head the golden chalice containing the menstrual blood of a dye job.

Wednesday

I was walking down a street on the outskirts of the city. My eyes were burning from the smog and the noise made me dizzy, but not knowing how to fly that was the best I could do. Behind me, from out of the bustling traffic and gray smoke, I heard a firm, somewhat shrill voice: 'Hey, young man!'

Whoever it was had to speak up to be heard over the honking, the screeching of tires, the sirens, the trucks, and the incessant rumble of civilization. I have the habit of turning around when someone calls out to me from behind. I don't know why I do it: hardly anything good comes of it (no one runs after me to give me a letter, tell me I've won the lottery, hand me the deed to an island in the Pacific, or even invite me for a cup of coffee). Maybe I do it because I'm afraid of being hit or shot from behind: I am a product of this century. So I turned around. On one side of the street, one of those depressing apartment towers that vulgar urban life peddles to naïve and prolific families wedded to the dream of being homeowners was going up. Those buildings are grimy even before people move into them, the doors don't close properly, the moisture seeps through the walls, and the pipes leak; a lot of people jump out of the windows, which face other identical buildings, and commit suicide. Across from the soot-covered building there was a limestone wall, which was also dirty, and two old ladies were sitting on it talking. (Land has gotten so expensive in our city that there aren't any squares or parks left.)

'Hey, young man!' one of them repeated when I turned around.

Bits of plastic plants lined the wall (today's city planners place them on the pavement to satisfy people's love of nature).

It seemed like a unique scene, something you'd take a picture of: the two gray-haired old ladies sitting on a limestone wall surrounded by cars and traffic lights, trying their best – despite the noise, the floating gas molecules, and the smell of exhaust and chemical contaminants – to hold a conversation. They were poor but they were tidily dressed, and each had a purse at her side.

'Could you tell me if today is Wednesday or Thursday?' one of them, the one who had called out to me, asked as I walked over to them.

It was the most unusual question anyone had ever asked me. At first I was flustered: simplicity is a lost art.

'I think it's Wednesday,' I stammered.

'What did I tell you?' the woman who hadn't yet said anything decreed sternly. She immediately became tender. A semi rumbled by and the pavement seemed to shake. An ambulance was transporting someone, dead or alive, somewhere.

'We were arguing about whether today is Wednesday or Thursday,' the old lady explained. 'She was sure it was Thursday, and I told her it was Wednesday.'

'I was confused,' the other one conceded meekly. Her sparse, long, gray hair was curled at the ends. I don't know why, but a retired B-movie actress came to mind. It must be the influence of television. She had applied her lipstick carefully, and you could imagine that once upon a time she'd had thicker lips. She smiled in an innocent, humble way, like a woman long humiliated by life.

'You're always getting confused,' the first one complained,

though not meanly. Despite her hard shell, I think she protected the other one a little, maybe because there was something vulnerable about her.

'Would you like to sit down?' the first one asked me, and she quickly moved to the side, freeing a portion of wall. She took the trouble of brushing it off first, as if it were a chair. I accepted. Even though I had a hole in my socks, it seemed like a good idea to roll up my pants.

'We spend the mornings here,' the first woman reported, making me think of a picnic in the countryside. A big bus was occupying a portion of the sidewalk near us and belched a thick cloud of smoke. The bus came to a raucous halt. Men, women, and children got off. For some strange reason there was a pocket of wind in the subway entrance that made leaves, newspapers, and trash fly around. The newsstand was full of magazines; next to it, someone was selling candy and hot peanuts. The rest of the block was taken up by a gargantuan supermarket, like some antediluvian animal.

'That's right,' the other one added, 'we're here every morning, except on Fridays. On Fridays we go to church.'

Friday struck me as being as good a day as any other to go church.

'Would you like a sandwich?' the first woman asked, fishing out a white package from her nylon purse. 'We always get a little hungry at this time. Which reminds me, do you know what time it is?'

I don't have a watch, but I figured it was about 11:00 A.M. I was hungry, so I accepted the sandwich. It was ham and cheese. I ate fast. They ate more slowly; their teeth might have been giving them trouble. But watching me eat made them happy.

'You have to eat!' the first one proclaimed. 'That's what I always

117

tell my children, "You have to eat!" ' A truck carrying oxygen tanks rumbled by. Someone's dying, I thought.

'But you never see your children,' the other one pointed out, and then immediately regretted what she'd said.

'I do too,' said the first one, without conviction. 'They visit me twice a year, at Christmas and on my birthday. Do you like the sandwich?'

I said I did and was sorry I hadn't said so earlier.

'I don't have any children,' the other woman reported. 'And I ran away from the old people's home,' she confessed with mischievous glee.

'It's true,' the first woman corroborated. 'She ran away over a month ago. No one knows where she is.'

'No one knows where I am,' the second woman repeated, grinning. 'But they won't look for me. Who would look for me?'

'No one cares about old people,' said the woman who had spoken first.

I agreed. 'Or about young people,' I added.

They looked at me, curious and attentive.

'It's true,' said the first woman. 'I have a little water in my bottle. Do you want some?'

I said I did and she handed me the bottle and an unused paper cup. I was thirsty. A hundred and fifty people – if not more – started walking at the same time when the red Cyclops changed colors. I was afraid there would be a stampede. Just in case, I clung to the wall.

'But I like young people a lot,' added the first woman, the one who looked like a retired actress. 'They're full of good feelings, even though you wouldn't know it,' she observed.

'As if you'd know!' grumbled the other one at the exact moment when eighty-three cars set off, speeding down the road. In the distance I saw the smoke rising from a laboratory on the hill, as if from a volcano.

I returned the bottle to the first woman.

'Old people have to look out for themselves,' she mumbled.

'We do too,' I added.

'See what I mean?' said the woman who'd spoken second. 'Didn't I tell you this world is no good for young people? They have to run away too.'

'I ran away from home a few years ago,' I said, 'and no one looked for me.'

'But you're probably more suited to it,' replied the second woman, flirtatiously. 'When I had to climb over a wall I got a run in my stockings. In my only pair.'

'Don't worry; I'll get you another pair,' the first woman offered tenderly. 'I'll steal some from my stingy daughter-in-law, she has a lot of them.'

Hundreds of children on their way home from school wearing brown uniforms and gray socks were looking eager to cross the street, like restless, fearful little animals in the jungle getting ready to step, jump, or fly for the first time.

'But it was fun,' said the woman. 'They probably think I got lost or that I died.'

'This world is no good for anyone,' I thought out loud.

'Luckily, she has me. I bring her sandwiches every day,' the first one pointed out, speaking to me. 'People have to help one another.'

'That's right, people have to help each other,' I said.

'It's no problem for me to share my food with you,' the second one said.

Now the traffic was all backed up, and exasperated drivers leaned on their horns. The blasts, long and persistent or else short and compulsive, were deafening. Some drivers got out of their vehicles, looked behind them, looked ahead, and got back in. Oblivious to the commotion, the traffic signals continued working, the eyes changing from one color to another.

If you want, I can give you some chocolate,' the first woman told me. 'It's good against the cold, it's full of calories.'

I accepted.

'Young people have big appetites,' said the second woman.

'Especially on Wednesdays,' I added, just to say something.

They seemed to find that very convincing.

'She gets the days mixed up because her memory is no good,' the second one explained to me.

'That's not true, Clara,' the first one protested. 'I've only forgotten a few years of my life, not all of them. Anyway, anyone can confuse one day with another.'

'It happens to me all the time,' I said in her defense.

'A little order is important,' the other one said. 'Monday is Monday, Tuesday is Tuesday, and Wednesday is Wednesday. Even though the world is falling apart and no one looks after old people or young people, you have to keep track of what's going on.'

That seemed reasonable enough to me. And once in a while it's good to listen to reasonable things.

'Where do you sleep, young man?' the second woman asked me in a very friendly voice.

'Here and there,' I answered vaguely. 'One day in one place, the next somewhere else.'

'They don't let you sleep on the station platforms anymore,' said the second woman, sadly.

120

'Now that's a shame,' said Clara, indignant.

'Terrible,' I said.

The retired actress had opened her purse and was now holding a small map in her hand, one of those maps they give you for free in the subway. She put her finger on a certain spot.

'Since I ran away, I've been sleeping there, at an abandoned train station. There's a watchman, a very kind and caring man. He's afraid of losing his job because he's old and no one loves him. He lets me sleep on a bench, and he even lends me blankets. I don't think he'd mind if you want to sleep there once in a while.'

I thanked her sincerely.

'Well, I have to go now,' said the first woman. 'If it were Thursday, I could stay a little longer, but it's Wednesday.'

'You've already said that more than once, Clara,' said the second woman.

The traffic was still backed up and I didn't see a single bird in the sky.

The Bathers

The bathers, all of them women, would arrive with the first days of November. The month of November isn't always the same: the sun isn't always shining or the sand dunes shuddering. Some Novembers are airless and leaden, the clouds low and gray, and it isn't exactly hot. Other Novembers are breezy and full of light; the sun gives the sand along the water's edge a golden hue and just a few yards out from the shore fish jump, lustrous in the shimmering waters. In places, the water is clear and you can see the outlines of small fish that swim amid the floating manes of moss and green weeds and that grow up there, protected by the rocks at the bottom. It's very hard to tell those fish apart from one another: leaning over the jetty, I would try to predict which ones would survive. It was a pastime doomed to failure: if I managed to identify one fish because of a certain pattern on its tail or by the shape of its fin, the next day I had no way of knowing if that particular fish had disappeared, swallowed by a larger fish, or whether it had simply left for other waters, having chosen another part of the sea to grow in. Knowing that this was a melancholy activity doomed to failure didn't prevent me from observing the fish for hours on end and running down the jetty when they suddenly decided to swim away. I found the water nearly as fascinating as the sudden movements of the fish. (Later, with time, I would discover other melancholy activities certain to fail; I met men and women determined to carry out impossible tasks, which to me seemed like the only really worthwhile ones.) The little fish swam in schools. Only the bigger ones dared to lead solitary lives and, although they were harder to spot, I was also interested in them. I was captivated by that secret, mysterious underwater world, by its silence, its continual movement, its hidden currents, and I think that was when I perceived, when I came to understand, that parallel universes exist, that the life we lead is only one among various possibilities and while ours – that of my family, my friends, the bathers – was lived on the surface and subject to certain rules and constraints, a lot of other completely discrete worlds also existed, even though we know nothing about them. This realization dominated my childhood and made me alternately happy and unhappy. As the little fish glided through the water experiencing stages of a life I couldn't fully observe or understand, I would wonder how many parallel worlds existed, even if I couldn't find a trace of any of them in a drop of water, a reflection, a fluttering wing, or a sudden gust of air.

Major changes in sensibility are rare. It is unlikely that more than three or four instances in the course of human history could be identified. For me, life next to the sea was the source of my emotions, of my feelings, the origin of my reflections, the only form of anxiety-free solitude I ever experienced. When I recall some of those summers – the strange, unpredictable month of November always foreshadowing the very different, inebriating light of January and the reddish explosion of February with its chattering crickets and pine trees scorched by the sun – I think that was the only time in my natural life when I was truly in touch with the elements: I crawled like an iguana, imitated the call of birds (they answered me from high branches), familiarized myself with the ways of crustaceans and mollusks, and collected bones, driftwood, and seaweed. I only had to raise my head to smell the storms, I recognized the sound of the wind from a long way away, and I slept among the rocks, like a crab. I knew when the corbinas would be in heat and discovered the iridescence (the illuminations) of bacteria.

What I liked about the month of November was its unpredictable nature. At the beginning of the month, I would see the schools of corbinas swimming by in search of warmer waters where they would couple and reproduce. It was the easiest time to catch them, especially the big ones. They would come close to the shore, I could see their silver backs rising and then submerging as they played, hear the slapping of the water, follow their successive leaps. I thought it was cruel and tragic that it was easiest to catch them when they were in heat, just as they were innocently playing their nuptial games. Later I discovered – and was able to confirm through personal experience – that being in heat isn't the opposite of dying and that there may even be a mutual attraction between these activities. But at the time I didn't know anything about Greek mythology.

The corbinas would swim past and sometimes, also in November, sea lions would wash up on the beach. They were big and had shiny black skin. There was something moving about their slick, clumsy bodies; it wasn't just their obscure desire to come and die on the shore. As the seagulls and all the other birds squawked and fluttered about, they could be on the verge of death for days. They had a hard time dying. Even though they could only move their heads, which they would drum against the sand, death came to them very slowly, in stages, and they waited for it lying down, as

124

if they didn't know what to do with their bodies, as if they were being crushed by a heavy weight.

This cruel, inexplicable spectacle disturbed me. In the bluish loneliness of the beach (those November days were opaque) I sensed a secret harmony among the giant dying sea lions, the lilac-colored clouds, and the ocher sea foam that drifted gently toward the shore. The throes of death, the squawking of bluebirds, the sound of the wind in the forest.

In the middle of November, the bathers would arrive. They would get off their shiny rented bus, chirping like confused birds, and hurriedly put on their bathing suits and caps. They exchanged creams, towels, and sandals, and bounded across the sand in play.

Their arrival that first time felt like a barbarian invasion. A blind rage, like that of the savage against the colonizer, welled up inside of me. I had never seen a group of people arrive at the beach. At first, I would hide behind the rocks and watch them suspiciously, hoping that the rain, an unexpected storm, or an accident (someone had told me about a gigantic wave that had once swept across that very spot and whose aqueous embrace covered the entire beach) would make them flee like a retreating army, abandoning stores and ammunition.

When I would walk alone along the shore, collecting shells and fossils, finding the small holes dug by clams, or searching for pearly talismans expelled by the sea, I had never felt the place belonged to me. It was such a vast expanse of sand, with pine trees mixed in among the eucalyptus further back; the sea stretched so far, to the East and West; there were so many trees, so many dunes, so much kelp; the jetties extended into the sea in such a lonesome way; the purple and brown rocks provided so many vincible barriers washed over by the waves that I didn't feel the need to possess the place. I was part of the landscape and subject to its allure.

But the presence of the bathers disturbed me. They represented an unmistakably human element in what, until then, had been only water, wood, rocks, mollusks, sounds, and movement. It wasn't just the animal instinct of territoriality in me that had been offended; it was the painful feeling that the harmony of the landscape had been disturbed, that the secret structure governing the maritime and vegetable kingdoms had been undone.

What I hated most that November when the women bathers showed up was the unexpected, imposing way they appeared. I felt betrayed for not having foreseen their arrival and also for being defenseless in the face of it. Before, the occasional visitors hadn't bothered me. I saw them in the distance, slowly walking along the beach, sometimes drawing in their limbs from the wind, and they were like those tiny, dark boats that would appear some afternoons, distant and austere, in the vastness of the sea. They fit in harmoniously with the landscape, like fossils, like Venus' belly button, like petrels seen in silhouette.

With the bathers, it was different. Laden with bags, picnic baskets, hats, towels, and suntan lotion, they arrived on a rented bus. This implied an intention to stay, in contrast to the comings and goings of the boats or the occasional, almost illusory strollers.

Like the ruler of an invaded country who knows he lacks the means with which to retaliate, I hid among the rocks and resentfully observed the activities of the barbarians.

The November days came and went, and with the beginning of December the situation remained unchanged: the bathers would arrive on their rented bus, file off of it laughing and playing and carrying their bags and bathing suits. They rubbed oil on their

126

skin and passed the days strolling, taking dips in the water and dozing on the sand, eating and drinking. I had no interest in knowing who they were or what they did. Like a suspicious peasant, I watched them from a distance, never coming close or betraying my presence.

In vain, I awaited the gigantic wave. Although I'd never seen one, I looked for the hint of such a wave on the horizon, tried to feel its birth in the depths of the sea where the ocean currents stir up stones and beds of grass. I was certain it would be swift and overwhelming, a torrential pyramid of water crashing down, rushing across the sand, the rocks, and the timid corral reefs. Its onslaught would change the structure of things forever. Sand would be lost, trees smashed, rocks displaced, slate platforms inundated, dunes destroyed. But that November the wave never struck, nor did it in December. The former order it was to have restored – through its very violence – was not obtained.

At the end of December, they stopped coming. Like primitive man, I discovered there were accidents and cycles over which neither my will nor desire held any sway. January came with its intense heat, the rustling of the pine trees, the chatter of the cicadas, the glimmer of the sand, the phosphorescence of the water, and I forgot about the bathers, like one can forget a storm, a bolt of lightning, or a squall.

The next year, in November, they were back. Although I was unhappy about this, I was less perturbed and saw that their presence was part of a cycle I would have to accustom myself to, just like fish, stars, insects, and plants adapt to things. This allowed me to feel a little more comfortable with their presence. At most, their interference would last a month or two. So I stopped hiding and although I didn't go near them, they must have noticed me often enough, even though they paid no attention to me. To them, I must have seemed like part of the landscape, like a tree trunk in the forest, a rock in the shape of a tower in the water, the glimmering lights that appeared in the sea at dusk, a cliff, or seashells calcified by the sun.

Just before the arrival of the fourth November, I discovered, to my surprise, that I was awaiting their arrival somewhat anxiously. Little had changed around me, so the change must have occurred within me, without my even noticing it. During the winter prior to what would have been the fourth November with the bathers, I began to feel slightly restless, uncomfortably lonely, and I avoided taking my usual strolls along the beach to contemplate the sea and the birds in flight. I was making more frequent trips to the city. I would walk the streets, look at shop windows, see a movie, or have a cold drink at a neon-lighted café whose secret charm had only just been discovered. I felt lonely in the city too, but contemplating the cars (I'll never forget the elegant, sinuous way the Buicks, which appeared for the first time that year, made their way down the city streets); the hiss of the espresso machines; the captivating music on the radio, those dark boxes where in exchange for a coin you could select a melody by pushing the keys of a shiny alphabetical code; the marquees advertising foreign films; and the platforms full of passengers, smoke, and used tickets made me forget that inside I was vaguely ill at ease.

November arrived with the imperious precision of the tides, of storms, of bouts of depression. It was a melancholy November: winter had gotten a late start and now it was lingering on as an unpredictable, cold, heavy spring. The wind was making the dunes tremble and I could see the mountains of sand shifting, like part of a barren lunar landscape. That year no sea lions came to die on the shore, and the only interesting thing I found was an old abandoned boat, in the bottom of which, motionless, were some rotting nets, ropes, and reddish floats. A sea gull (I don't know if it was always the same one) would perch on one end of the boat. Serene and impervious, like a figurehead at the prow, it would watch over the horizon.

One afternoon, while contemplating the hypnotic calm of the slate-gray sea and a few lilac-colored clouds strewn across the horizon, I realized that I was somehow awaiting the arrival of the bathers. I was doing nothing else as I walked over the mountains of sand, poked around in the forest in search of a late mushroom, or carved on tree trunks the outlines of birds swooping down over the water to swallow a fish. The tall trees shuddered in the wind, and the color of the sky vaguely augured storms.

Toward the end of November I began to suspect that, unlike in previous years, the bathers wouldn't come. The feeling that a cycle had been interrupted, broken by some mysterious chance event, left me bitterly uneasy. The good thing about the cycles is that they diminished my sense of vulnerability, of instability, offering me guidelines, a certain feeling of order I could cling to. There was something naïve and obvious about them. The breaking of the cycle, on the other hand, introduced an element of chaos, an incomprehensible phenomenon that perturbed me and, worse still, excluded me, giving me no chance to intervene.

I decided to go to the city to look into this. I didn't know anything about the bathers, just the time of year they arrived, when they left, and that they came and went on a rented bus. In the city, I went to the bus company. It was a company that organized day trips to different places. They had no fixed schedule, and the destination was determined by the passengers themselves and the price negotiated. After a lot of pleading, I was able to see the records from the previous year, which included several excursions to the beach. But there was no mention of the names of the bathers, what they did for a living, or even where they came from. I found it very strange that there was no sign saying 'Bathers' Bus,' or something to that effect. I couldn't ask for them because I didn't know who they were. It was as if the city had scattered them like petals in the wind. I was so devastated that outrageous ideas occurred to me. I thought the bathers might have all grown old and that they no longer thought it looked good to go to the beach. With my prior lack of interest in them, I hadn't even noticed the age of the women. I gave it a try: I pictured them at the moment they were getting off the bus all loaded down with bags and towels, and they seemed like a choir of boisterous girls. Yet, as I recalled them happily jumping into the water – splashing one another like birds in a fountain – or sprawled under the sun, motionless like lazy reptiles, their ages seemed to vary. Could they have grown old so rapidly, been struck by a strange disease? I tried to find more reasonable explanations: some of them might have gotten married, others changed jobs, two or three of them moved from the city so there weren't enough of them left to fill up the bus. Although this explanation was more plausible than the first, it still left me in a state of paralyzing dismay. I couldn't accept the idea that the group had broken up. I refused to recognize the individuality of its members. For me, they constituted a group, a unity with an indivisible, collective fate. They arrived at the beach together on the bus before noon and left together at dusk, without any of their trivial personal activities – combing their hair, using their towels to dry off their backs, applying suntan lotion – endowing them with individuality. I couldn't accept the idea that

130

one might have gotten married, betraying the rest of them, or that another might have left her job. I'd never stopped to think what they did when they left the beach or during the winter, but I secretly imagined that they stayed together, that they worked at the same place (that maybe they were all teachers at a school in the outskirts of the city or that they were typists at the same firm), that they were all of about the same age and lived together. If not all in the same house (such big houses no longer existed), at least in groups of four or five and in the same neighborhood. It was extremely upsetting to imagine the appearance of a foreign element in the group, a man for instance, a dog, a trip abroad, or a change of profession.

Suddenly, I realized that the assumptions I'd taken for granted must have been wrong and that instead of reflecting reality, they reflected my own fantasies about the bathers. This disturbed me and ushered in a period of new reflections about the tendency to substitute imagination for analysis. From then on, I began to feel insecure every time I thought I knew something.

That November, walking along a beach that felt completely deserted, whose loneliness distressed me, I began to experience self-doubt. I was certain I would betray myself more than once. I would have given anything to see that bus pull up one morning with the light glinting off its shiny metal body, to hear the confused chatter of the women's voices, to see them venture into the water amid their shrieks of surprise and halting jumps.

They didn't come. The cycle had been broken, and I was uncertain whether it would ever be restored.

Notes on a Journey

You have to travel a long way, in the Krupp Family Gallery, to find the seaside landscape painted by Salomon van Ruysdael – the luxuriant trees bowed by the wind (yet the landscape is remarkable for its tranquility; the wind that bent the branches and made the leaves flutter was blowing on some previous day, at some time in the past), the Gothic church in the distance, the dark boat ferrying sheep, the sailing vessels setting off for silver-blue waters. But no one makes such a long journey just to see a painting. So it turns out that the traveler who went to the city for other reasons discovers the painting, and when he remembers it, in the silence of a dark room or in a park where children play with balloons, he is astonished by the infinite combination of chance events that led him to the city; that thought – occurring to him at some moment in the afternoon – makes him suddenly realize that van Ruysdael arranged the clouds, gave the sail a reflection, and made the castle tower fade in the distance out of an utter fear of chaos, otherwise known as chance.

The traveler who suddenly discovered the van Ruysdael painting may be the same one who, later, at dusk, sitting at an outdoor table of a *Konditorei* in Berlin, writes the following on a postcard:

My love,

Chance precludes certainty. Having said that, I should add that on occasion a little certainty – glimpsed like the silvery light in a painting – is so intense that for a time (say, for the period from the end of childhood until old age) it imposes order on chaos. I love you with the force of one of those rare illuminations.

She didn't see the van Ruysdael painting; in fact the postcard, improperly stamped, didn't arrive and the illumination is apt to disappear at any moment. But since the traveler is unaware of these facts, he combs the cities for images, reflections, episodes, and small mementos to take to his beloved so that she – in her imagination, without leaving home – can reconstruct the journey.

Despite the pain attending the revelation that she doesn't love him and may never have loved him, the traveler knows that his brief contemplation of the painting was of an intensity comparable only to that of an obsession. Like Gulliver, he hopes to undertake another journey and is confident of finding another painting.

In an old bookshop in Chinatown, he finds and is shaken by the following passage in a book:

The complicity with which they look at a painting, walk through the streets, contemplate an Italian garden, or purchase a book gleams like crystal and is as fragile and breakable as its own reflection; it floats above the earth before bursting, but it did fly above the waters, linger at the top of a tree, and produce numerous visions.

★

133

In his dreams, he forms part of that couple.

I have noticed that in some cities they serve small amounts of tea in a simple glass accompanied by sugar cubes. The scant amount of liquid and the informality with which it is served seem to suggest the tea should be drunk in a hurry, before taking one's leave as quickly as possible, as if one had done something wrong. Elsewhere, however, they serve it in fine porcelain cups decorated with delicate arabesque motifs, golden flowers, and eighteenth-century landscapes that are echoed in the saucers. The sugar (granulated) is served in a matching bowl. The teapot has a metal top. The liquid is like a vessel floating in a calm sea, and from the cup flow numerous memories and digressions. The infusion encourages one to stay, to linger, to contemplate the cupola of the church, to listen to the rustle of the trees.

He remembers two fascinating mermaids: one rises by the sea in Sitges, next to the church, the other is inside a café in Berlin, and its image is replicated in the motif on the napkins and cups.

The Mediterranean is a calm sea, but the waves crash against the angle formed by the church and the jetty (from the far side of which rises a light house). A grand staircase leads down to the esplanade, which runs along the water's edge. The water is flanked by rocks that, like a set of blocks left behind by a forgetful child, have perfectly straight edges. The church, the staircase, the jetty, and the bollard make up a truly singular whole, and he wonders if this curious composition is the result of chance or of a carefully calculated plan. The mermaid is there, her back to the sea, touching her head with a gracefully raised hand.

No one knows the age of mermaids, if some of them are pubescent and others all grown up, or whether they reach old age. (He seems to remember the disturbing sight of an old mermaid in a painting by Böcklin.) The little mermaid in Sitges, in any case, is a young mermaid: she has arisen from the sea as if from an earthenware bowl; she is concerned with the state of her hair and would like to look at herself in a mirror. Children light up the night around her with flares. Stars of color explode, fireworks blossom above the boats; she is part of the festivity, as if her bronze-colored tail were an elegant dress she had put on for a costume party.

In contrast, the mermaid in Berlin suffers the consequences of her dual identity, which tears her apart and makes her languish. Humiliated by the false tail that imprisons her legs, she feels a nostalgia for movement that, paradoxically, draws attention to the fact that she is reclining. The tail binds her, fuses her to the shore whence she came while her face (green, like kelp) recalls the melancholy of the sea. She rose painfully from the depths of the ocean (which is brown and earthen-colored). She still has the painful stigmata from the ascent: sea horses, starfish, and strands of seaweed are caught in her hair, appearing not so much like adornments as the shameful marks that perverse men inflict on one another.

She rests one exhausted hand on the ground, the other is raised slightly in an imploring gesture. Like someone trapped for life in an undersized suit of armor, she bends her midsection slightly to relieve the discomfort. Only her forward movement suggests that the flight has begun and that, like a chrysalis, she is about to shed her tail in the backroom of the Berlin café.

★

He knows that he is doomed to travel, to comb the images of bridges, lakes, and canals, cobblestone streets, and old train stations with patterned rooftops for the symbols of an ambiguous condition, like that of the mermaids. He also knows that any journey through space is also a journey through time and through the transposed figure that that double journey evokes, he is confident of finding – in the port of a city he has never visited or on the platform where trains are departing in various directions at once – echoes of her at other moments in time, in other places, just as he found them in the van Ruysdael painting, in an old book, in a postcard, in the happy mermaid in Sitges, in the tormented mermaid in a Berlin café.

The City

The dream came back to him time and again. In it, there was an unidentifiable presence – *someone* of indeterminate sex whose face he couldn't see but who was clearly there. The dream wasn't quite the same every time (certain physical aspects changed; sometimes it was day, sometimes night; there was a house, but not always the same house, or there was no house at all and the surface of the dream was as desolate as a pampa), but upon awakening he was certain that those discrepancies were immaterial: the atmosphere of the dream, its climate, was the same. And always the memory – or, rather, the foreboding – that there was someone in the dream whose face he couldn't see, a mysterious presence, that almost certainly held the key to the dream's meaning, without which he was left full of doubt, defenseless, because not knowing the nature of our dreams is a sort of self-betrayal, a perilous trap set by the forces within.

Most recently, he conjured up a city he knew – he had been born there thirty-six years ago but had left at the age of twenty – and although in the dream he *knew* that that was the city he was from, so many things had changed there that it had become unrecognizable. Yet still, in his dream, he knew it was the city where he had been born. If dreams could be photographed (the fact that man had made it to the moon but still couldn't manage to remember all of his dreams was a contradiction that gave rise to a lot of ironic thoughts), surely he would be able to say what had allowed him to recognize the city, despite its altered appearance.

That distant city, where his dreams took him on a journey he'd never intended to undertake, was and was not the same, and his presence there only served to bring about a feeling of strangeness and, at the same time, of recognition, not unlike what happens when one looks at an old photograph. But a camera always captures a moment from the past, and he couldn't be certain whether the city he saw in his dreams was part of the past, the present, or the future: it was a different city, to be sure, and it floated in a space detached from time, from geographic or chronometric exactitude, in a space yet to be created, that was suspended from something that wasn't memory but that likewise wasn't a premonition. Surely, the city where he was born was not like that, hadn't been like that, nor would it be like that; but in his dream it was his city. He was therefore the architect of a city he hadn't wanted to build, that surprised him with its steep ravines, high meadows, symmetrical windows, and mercurial afternoon light (there were wells full of water and some black birds resembling crows but that weren't crows). The city surprised him with its squares – deserted save for the statues – its expanse of streets without houses, and its enormous clock that had fallen to the ground and that always indicated an unlikely time of day. Whether he was in one of those squares, touching the cold marble of the statues or trying, in vain, to find a taxi (he had to go somewhere – he didn't remember where, but he was certain it was elsewhere, perhaps on another continent, somewhere under a different sky), or else trying to scale a rotating mountain (like papier-mâché models at an amusement park, the mountains moved), he was always aware of

138

a strange presence; there was someone else, he couldn't remember who, someone he may not have known but that was there, behind his back or to one side, an invisible, expressionless figure that dominated his dream and the town squares of his dream. Had he made the journey in the company of the stranger or was the figure already there, waiting for him in the city he'd quit at the age of twenty, fleeing chaos and madness?

Once, he'd discovered a patio from the neighborhood of Alcoé in his dream and this discovery gave him a feeling of familiarity. Within the dream itself he had felt the satisfaction of recognition, as if having seen the round patio with its large blue and white mosaics of parallel geometric figures, and the green plants in their sumptuous gray pots (like those in the house of his ancestors – ficus and bougainvillea against the white wall of the back patio), had restored his sense of confidence, as if it were a missing link in the chain he had to assemble, even though he was feeling weak and impotent and sorry for himself. On another occasion it was a window. He was certain that that window, with its delicate transparent curtains through which you could make out a piece of a mauve-colored Gobelin and the rounded leaf of a table (probably used as a telephone stand), was the window onto a room he had known as a child and had visited frequently to play with the girl with golden braids and thick red lips, the girl who was his childhood companion. (He didn't dream about the girl, but the window made him evoke her and for two days he longed to send her a letter, a postcard, anything that would attest to his existence, which was separated from hers by thousands of miles and, even worse, by dozens of years irretrievably gone by.)

But if the Alcoé patio – a stone's throw from the train station built by the English (whose old, majestic ironwork that, as he remembered it, still recalled the frames and scaffolding of a shipyard; for him it was unimportant whether the station was for trains or boats) – and the window in Miraflores (where he had lived and grown up aimlessly until setting out on the journey that would once and for all take him far away because he had no desire to participate in one of those collective, uncontrollable, contagious acts of insanity that engender catastrophes) were solid facts, oars with which to ply the tempestuous seas of his strange dream, pillars of an enigmatic building (the city) built by unknown hands, there were other details that, given the difficulty of connecting them to any known reality, filled him with uncertainty. The mountains spun and the trees had blue leaves; the surface of the earth was petrous – sometimes – and a few thick, dark, human hairs sprouted from the rocks. There were no cars crossing the barren plateau, and the port had suddenly disappeared. As strange as an urban landscape devoid of cars, revolving doors, or elevators was his simultaneous feeling of belonging and not belonging to the place. No one recognized him, which surprised him, even though he himself recognized no one. Sometimes they took him for a foreigner, other times for someone who had always lived there. The city was burdened by a big secret. That much he could make out in the dream; a secret that was a burden to him as well and that he was afraid to divulge inadvertently. But sometimes he forgot altogether what the secret was, which only heightened his anxiety.

And always, at one point or another in the dream, the feeling that an unknown (or simply unrevealed) presence was following him – not with the intention of making him feel less alone or vaguely protected but for reasons of its own. It was there, but it wasn't clear since when; it had an obscure relationship to him, a relationship he had forgotten, and one of his failings – not his only failing but his greatest – was precisely that he couldn't say what that relationship was.

He was certain that once, in his dream, he had discovered the gender of the presence. This discovery filled him with excitement as he slept, but upon awakening the certainty disappeared. It didn't fade, it vanished, overshadowed by diurnal reality. Though he struggled like a surgeon trying to extract the mysterious poison from the inscrutable viscera or like a collector of clams who buries his hand in a hole to grab a shell, he couldn't summon from the dark well of his memory, couldn't bring to the surface again, couldn't pull the revelation – again submerged in uncertainty – to shore. He became annoyed with himself, and he cursed the impotence, the weakness of the diurnal mind. He attempted to go back to sleep (although experience dictated otherwise, he had the secret hope of again dreaming the same thing and recovering that part of the dream that the light of day kept from him), and when he did, he floated on opaque cavernous waters that rocked him like a cork at sea.

It was then that it occurred to him to try doing things the other way around. If the dream wouldn't reveal the secret, if the anonymous presence was unwilling to identify itself, he would have to search for the sign, the solution to the nocturnal enigma, in reality. Surely something in the people he knew, in the people who made up his universe, would provide that revelation. He had gone about it the wrong way: rather than probing the sinuosities of his dream, its rarefied atmosphere, he should search through the elements of daily life. He was certain it was something subtle that he hadn't noticed before. People are often inattentive, imperceptive, ritualistic in relating to those around them. The plethora of

141

objects between each of us and others form a barrier and condemn us to solitude, the oasis and burial ground of our aspirations. Often the cup of tea we offer the visitor is not only an act of courtesy but also a way of establishing a barrier that demarcates our respective spaces. And it's easier for us to accept an infringement on the part of the vine out on the balcony (it has begun climbing through the window) than on that of the visitor who has dared to stay an extra half hour at our house (ossuary).

From the outset he discarded the more trivial figures: neighbors, colleagues at the office, casual acquaintances with whom his relationship was as cordial as it was superficial: none of them could have gained access to his dream because doing so would have required possessing a secret, making enough of an impression on the membranes of his memory. Once the extraneous figures had been ruled out, he was astounded at how short the list was. It became clear to him that in recent years (possibly since the age of thirty) he had, almost unconsciously, endeavored to surround himself with benign, inconsequential presences that didn't involve love and with whom he could share a glass of wine or a pastry without committing himself to anything, with whom he could go to the movies or play pool without revealing any intimacies. Figures that were complacent in their own quiescence, with whom he might have had only one thing in common: the dreamless dream of daily life, the unruffled passage of the day-to-day, the routine where one hides out of fear of anything unknown. At most, he had spoken with them about the need for a fallout shelter, like in the most advanced countries, a new need that might serve as a substitute for the house in the countryside or at the beach.

Once the inconsequential figures had been ruled out, there

142

were only a couple of people left to investigate as possible spectres in his dreams, and he promised himself he would do so with the utmost care.

First he thought of Luisa, whom he hadn't seen for a long time. They had been married for a few years and, although the marriage had been a failure, he retained a vague sense of guilt, as if the failure had been his fault, the result of something he should have given her but, for lack of an incentive, didn't – as if needing an incentive were in itself a culpable need. His tangled web of guilt had led to immoderate acts whose very exaggeration renewed his feelings of guilt, and from an unbridgeable distance, far from a stage full of lights, she witnessed those twists and turns, the imprisoning responsibilities, as if they were the balancing act of a tightrope walker. Luisa had never been with him in his native city: obscurely and unwaveringly certain that on the other side of the ocean lay a different world full of lethal plagues, poisonous foods, frightening creatures, wild animals, angry volcanoes, raging rivers, and a general lack of hygiene, she had strong feelings of rejection toward non-European countries. The long conversations they'd had in which he tried to convince her that things *were not exactly like that* ran up against a resistance that was more instinctual than rational, as if Luisa wanted to protect herself from an enormous danger that she had placed beyond the ocean so that she could live safely and comfortably on her side.

'I dreamed about the city again, Luisa,' he told her when they met at a downtown café. He made the confession timidly, like a child who had repeated a mistake he had already been punished for.

She looked at him disconcertedly. For a long time it had been difficult for her to look directly at people. She had gone to the ophthalmologist who prescribed glasses, but that didn't solve the problem: now the light bothered her, both daylight and artificial light, and she struggled to focus on small objects – scraps of paper, pencils, pencil sharpeners, anything that sat on the surface of things and that, unlike faces, didn't move.

'It's that same dream, Luisa,' he continued, certain he was barreling down a naked hillside, the bottom of which was nowhere in sight, and certain all the same that he would not try to grab onto anything he might find on the way. His friend Juan called it annihilation vertigo. The condition afflicted some members of the world and was apparently incurable.

'But in the dream, there's a presence. I wasn't sure about this before (and Luisa didn't know if he meant a few months ago or that period during their marriage, that ambiguous time when both of them felt they were drifting helplessly like seaweed, fearfully scrutinizing themselves and being otherwise unable to focus on superficial, everyday things). Before, I sensed something strange – not just in the appearance of the city – but I didn't know what it was. Now I know (I've been certain about this for a while) that it's a presence, someone who appears in the dream even though I don't see a face or a body but that is there, in the city, like my own shadow. I don't know if the presence made the journey with me or whether it was there waiting for me (and sometimes, Luisa, I don't even think the journey takes place: sometimes I've never gone away or, inexplicably, I'm there, without having left, regardless of whether I'm going or staying – they're mere words, without any substance); I don't know if the presence prompts me to return or whether I drag it with me. But the presence experiences no anxiety or confusion. It's there and I don't know what it feels or wants, it has a certain power over me. Beyond the powers I suspect it has is the ability to become dark, to hide its identity, to resist my efforts to catch it in the light of day. I don't know who it is, if it's a man or a woman.'

She made an effort to look at his face without blinking. She wasn't certain whether he was really speaking to her. She wasn't certain whether he had ever spoken to her. What was wrong with him that he could only address symbols? Interchangeable symbols: if she were Inés rather than Luisa, he would have made the same revelations; it didn't matter whether her hair was dark or golden; it didn't matter that she found his dreams repellent, that that world seemed to her as distant and inhospitable as the one that was on the other side of the ocean, of that vainglorious ocean that separated them, because the function of the ocean was always the same – to differentiate them.

With great effort she looked at him (his features were, however, not exotic as she always thought they should be) to determine just how complete her rejection was. What did he want from her? She was tired. She had worked all day and longed for a bath, soft music, strawberry yoghurt. There's nothing like strawberry yoghurt when you're tired. And out of the bath onto a plush white mat that caressed her so softly she could stay there all night, protected by its warmth. A night that he would doubtless spend exploring his dream, like a diver.

'Have you thought about returning?' she asked him, and he felt a shiver down his spine.

He looked straight at her, for the first time, as if she had just appeared there in her elegant tailored suit and blouse with its pastel-colored ruffles, with her long delicate hands that at times gave him the irresistible urge to kiss them. But the question had inexplicably hurt him.

'No, Luisa, I'm not talking about *that* city, don't you under-stand? It's not a matter of returning anywhere. Or of going any-where. Maybe people who aren't foreigners don't carry a city inside them,' he thought aloud. 'They don't dream about unfamil-iar maps.'

'You've lived in this city for long enough to have adapted by now,' she said harshly. She too felt vaguely hurt and thought to herself that those were the things that in the end distanced people from one another – vague wounds, sores, rivalries.

Suddenly he had the urge to leave. Something, like a street glimpsed in the middle of a dream (a winding street with leaning buildings, mildewed walls, glimmering wet pavement), attracted him, but to where he couldn't say.

It was different with Juan, who had just returned from a trip to the city where they were both born. He decided to submit him to rigorous questioning (a euphemism common in police reports, with which they were both all too familiar). But Juan had returned melancholy and uncommunicative. He replied in monosyllables; nothing interested him so much as reenacting the Battle of Water-loo on the living room floor after work, and he refused to engage in discussions that concerned time or space.

'We must unite!' was his rallying cry as he got off the plane slightly lightheaded. He hated flying – the stewardesses made him strangely nervous ('I'll never believe them,' he declared), and he couldn't tolerate the absence of asphalt beneath his feet. Rather than telling him what he was expecting to hear (even though he couldn't say just what that was, he was certain he would recognize it if he heard it), Juan recounted in minute detail the various catas-trophes that almost occurred during the sixteen-hour flight and even described all of the passengers and their minor eccentricities. Days went by and Juan seemed increasingly engrossed in the Battle of Waterloo; he was certain he could change the outcome, and he continually said that it was the only change an individual could effect on history: there on the carpet, with toy soldiers.

'Juan, I dreamed about the city again,' he reported one afternoon, taking advantage of a break in the game. In order to concentrate better, Juan played alone, against himself. 'My left hand doesn't know what my right hand is doing,' he would say, 'and because my memory is as poor as that of most peoples of the world, I immediately forget massacres and acts of injustice, reinstate ousted generals, decorate traitors, return fallen soldiers to their positions on the battlefield, bomb the cities – with remarkable impunity.'

Juan aimed carefully at a fortress, deployed a lieutenant general, and advanced three spaces. Napoleon's army was retreating. 'Imagine,' he said, 'when I got back, I'd forgotten that the street corners here are oblique, I thought they met at a right angle, like ours. This made for confusion while walking around. A car that was turning almost ran me over. Foreigner dead in the middle of the street. There's something indecent about dying in a place that isn't one's own. Only natives should die. The bodies of foreigners get left around for other people to take care of. And you know, darling, xenophobia is on the rise. So much for that damned English captain!' Juan exclaimed, whisking the arrogant soldier off the board.

'There are some statues in the city that I'd never seen before,' he interrupted, as if revealing a secret.

'Do you think people ever look at statues?' Juan asked. 'They're created precisely so that people won't look at them. At the same time, a city without statues would be inconceivable. Do you know if there are any statues in Amsterdam? I don't know much about the philosophy of lacustrine cities.'

'What's strange about those statues,' he continued, 'is that they always have their back to me so I can't identify them. Going over and seeing their faces ought to solve the problem, but in my dream something prevents me from doing that. The street is too steep, the square is broken or, to my surprise, I have to climb a difficult staircase that, in any case, leads nowhere.'

'The city looked hopelessly flat to me,' Juan added. 'Of course, you know there are no mountains, hills, or even tall buildings there, but the *sensation* of flatness was almost unbearable. I thought of Gulliver. I would climb anything just to experience the feeling of height. Sometimes, in the elevator, I found myself trying to encourage the contraption to go a few floors higher. And the houses have no more than three or four stories and there are no other possibilities: that's the way it is, my friend, you have to accept it.'

'The other night, for a moment, I seemed to know the name of the city. I had asked a sailor who was walking down the street (oddly, though, the port had disappeared). He told me the name but it didn't register with me. And you know? He repeated it, but it didn't register.'

'It might not have meant anything,' said Juan, as he cautiously launched an artillery attack. The game was occupying most of the livingroom floor, and anyone walking across the room would need to do so with great care, to avoid crushing an army division or one of the French tankers departing from the port of Calais.

'It must have been a clue,' he insisted.

'There's a reason why you forgot it. Either it was unimportant

148

(I hate that tendency to focus on the most insignificant things – we should respect the right of venial things to exist) or else it was so important that you blocked it out. Choose whichever of the two explanations suits you, in the same way that I, right now, will decide which of the armies should win. In any case,' he added, 'I have no doubt that the city you dream about has no connection with the one where you were born. I know this for a fact.'

He wanted a description, a precise, detailed description of the city Juan had found. But Juan didn't have the slightest urge to provide one. He demanded to be believed, as an act of faith.

'The presence,' he said, 'could be a man. Nothing leads me to believe that it is a woman.'

'Any sexual definition, my darling, strikes me as scandalous. We are the sex we were assigned; at best we accept it. Let's hope that in our dreams, if nowhere else, that definition ceases to prevail. Did I tell you that I'm dressing up as an old-fashioned lady at the next carnival? I've already bought the dress. I made up my mind on the plane, on the way back. We were flying at an altitude of twenty-one thousand feet. The emergency light was suddenly illuminated. The captain muttered a few unintelligible sentences from the flight deck, those unimportant things they say: "remain calm, everything is all right," and so on. That's always the moment when I start trembling. I realized we were making a dizzying descent, though I couldn't say why. And you know what thought popped into my mind? I remembered that when I was five I had wanted to dress up as an old-fashioned lady. Imagine how scandalized my family was. They left me with few alternatives: I had to choose between being an eighteenth-century French soldier or a fireman. What I wanted was to walk around under a lilac-colored parasol decorated with white flowers and put on a pair of fur-lined

149

muffs! It was very difficult for me to understand the strict prohibition. I attributed it to one of those absurd, inexplicable, arbitrary rules governing the life of adults. The plane recovered altitude and we could all breathe again. One passenger asked for a whisky, another for a box of cigars. Several others got up to go to the lavatory. The stewardess walked past me, and I swear I had the urge to ask her for a lilac-colored parasol and a pair of furry muffs. I'm used to living with big unsatisfied urges but I can't stand not giving in to the little ones. So as soon as I got off the plane (you know how I hate not being met at the airport, but in this city no one meets anyone) I went to a big department store and ordered an old-fashioned lady's dress tailor-made for me. It only needed a few minor alterations,' Juan said, happy with his clever description.

He didn't seem to be paying attention. 'I'd like to see some photographs,' he said humbly.

Juan gave him a look of reproach. He was about to lose his Norman spy, which would imply a new strategic dilemma. 'I didn't take any pictures, darling,' he replied brusquely. 'I can't stand necrophilia.'

Hesitantly, he went outside. He thought it was very dark. Time had probably gone by without his even noticing. He should have wished Juan luck in reconstructing the Battle of Waterloo. He was probably going to be able to change the course of history. The trees were bowed by the wind (though the wind never blows in this city, he mused), and the higher branches seemed to be spinning like carriage wheels. As soon as he stepped away from the threshold, he found a large open ditch he hadn't noticed before. It was full of dirt and stagnant, malodorous water smelling of wet and rotten grass. Where is the taxpayer's money going? he thought. He had to be careful not to sink his foot into the gulch. He walked on a few yards, along the narrow margin between the wall and the hole, and when he reached the corner he was surprised to discover that the bank building had been replaced by a small, two-story house with a garden on its flat roof. Buildings were quickly constructed and torn down in accordance with urban speculation but he couldn't understand how the solid, broad, powerful bank tower had been demolished so fast and then replaced by a simple provincial-looking house. The streetlight wasn't working properly and he preferred to cross to the other side in search of familiar walls. It was a city without cats, but when he crossed the street a couple of huge black felines almost scampered across his feet and hissed a discontented meow. Strangest of all was the absence of automobiles. There were none in sight either up or down the avenue, and he didn't think it could be so late that everyone was asleep. He didn't see any busses either, which only added to his confusion. He must be lost. But how had he gotten himself there? He couldn't see the street names – there were no signs or plaques – and that left him at even more of a loss. He looked for a phone booth. He wanted to call Juan and ask him for help. Despite his mocking air, Juan was a good friend. It was dark, but luckily he found a telephone a few steps away. Unlike the other phone booths in the city, which were red, this one was green, which he found disconcerting. All the same, he entered. The numerals had faded from the disk, which tends to happen with phones that have been used a lot. He wanted to dial the number three, but he suddenly realized that the dial was made of stone, immovable. He tried again, attempting to force it, but the dial refused to turn. With all his might he hit it, but to no avail. What kind of person would play a trick like that? He gave up and decided to try another phone. He didn't see one nearby. But now the ground was tilting steeply to one side, rising like the slope of a hill, and the trees were spinning. There was no one in sight, the city looked completely desolate, and the street lamps were dark. He tried to take another step (not in the direction of the hill, the other way), but his right foot sank into a shapeless glob of mud. When had it rained? His foot was stuck and he tried to pull it out. He looked up at the top of the mountain and, astonished, saw that it was rotating. The heavens, the trees, and the mountain were all rotating. And suddenly he felt there was a strange presence not far from him. He couldn't identify it in the darkness. The heavens, the trees, and the mountain were rotating, he couldn't get his foot out of the mud, the dial on the telephone was made of stone, and someone was there, not far from him, inscrutable, someone who neither came close nor moved away, someone whose blurry face he couldn't see (then how did he know that the face was blurry?), someone at once familiar and distant who didn't offer a handshake (did that someone have a hand?), an unknown man or woman, woman or man, whose oppressive presence buried him ever deeper in the mud of a street he didn't recognize and that perhaps wasn't even a street.

Casting Daisies to the Swine

I get up early to feed the pigs.

The fields are still dark, a big gray cloud is parked overhead, but the patch of white daisies flutters in the wind, resplendent. Over to the right is the wooden pen where the pigs, gray in the half-light of dawn, are sleeping. A strip of barren brown earth separates the field of daisies from the pigpen. I walk slowly back and forth from one end of the strip to the other, alternately looking at the shapely flowers, which are white with a dot of yellow in the center, and at the gray backs of the pigs that sleep wedged in against one another with their weird hoofs sticking out.

Once I've gathered enough daisies I go over to the pigsty, which is closed. Still clumsy with sleep, the pigs jostle and bump against one another and grunt like a distant thunderstorm when they see me coming.

The very early mornings are almost always gray. At that time of day, the daisy patch flutters in the wind, and the green flower stems bend over and almost touch the ground. The pigs raise their heads and squeal into the air. But then again they would probably do the same thing if instead of daisies they were going to be fed thistles. They trample their way over to the fence, the skin on their backs gray with a hint of salmon at the ends of the hairs, the sky languid and sprawling, the daisies rippling like a sea of yellow cork floats.

The wisdom of the daisies can be found in their stems, which are tough but flexible and manage to bend without decapitating the blossoms. The wisdom of the pigs, in contrast, is harder to identify. It's practically an impenetrable secret, not unlike that of stones or minerals. Innocent like children, brutal like the gods of former times, those big totems are far too heavy for their little, ridiculously coquettish feet, which explains the clumsiness of their movements and their frequently sullen gaze.

I toss my load of daisies over the fence; they fall as if dropped from space, like dozens of cadavers from a steam shovel into a pit. They fall silently, and the flowers – their necks snapped – scatter a yellowish dust across the ground. The earth is quickly covered by the dust, as if by a layer of sand that had just fallen as rain.

The round tops of the daisies being reduced to a yellow powder doesn't faze the pigs. Like surly baritones who ate too much, they squeal from their innermost, grease-coated viscera and jostle and push each other as they gobble up the broken green stems and white petals, which disappear down the dark hole of their snouts, as if being pulled to the bottom of the sea.

You have to pick a lot of daisies to satisfy the pigs. Sitting on top of the fence, I take in the spectacle with a certain feeling of melancholy, the pigs bumping into one another, devouring the daisies, their shrill blasphemous squeals. They would bustle around just like that if they were being fed thistles. But there's something beautiful – which they don't understand – about the fact that under this desolate gray sky they're eating daisies.

When they've finished eating the first bunch and they raise their snouts, all made-up with the yellow daisy dust, they clumsily look around for more and I run back over to the field to collect another load of daisies. If I didn't tend the field, there might be a shortage of daisies, and the flowers, with their beautiful white crowns, wouldn't flutter in the wind. But I look after the field, and the sky, which is permanently gray, helps me with its gentle rains, and the wind cooperates by scattering the seeds.

Once, when I was little (I was already taking care of the field), my mother peered out from the threshold of the house like a dark, unexpected apparition and scolded me. I was in the field, picking flowers in the cold wind when I suddenly saw her, a black figure on the stone and cardboard stage set.

'Son,' she said, 'why are you feeding daisies to the pigs?'

I looked at the flowers, which were gently fluttering in the wind and stretched out before my eyes, their yellow centers under the uniformly gray sky. It was a long field, and the flowers were arranged symmetrically. On the other side, the pigpen was round and a mist of sweat and dung and the penetrating smell of the clumsy sleeping totems wafted up. Few people can stand the smell, which, although I don't enjoy it, offers me limitless possibilities for research. There's something in there, among the garbage and jumbled-up things, that comes out of the past. I discover soggy roots, rotten tree trunks, digested dry grass, acidic juices secreted from deep viscera. A ball of stink kneaded together with slimy, sordid liquids.

My mother could also see the big field of daisies jagged against the gray sky, like an island of pelicans glimpsed between the waves by a castaway. And she could see the muddy pigs, wallowing together in their vulgar but innocent lasciviousness.

'It's a big field,' I told her. 'I've only planted daisies, I don't think there's anything else growing there. I pick the daisies and they grow back again. The secret of the daisies is that they don't know themselves, which gives them their beauty and humility.'

The pigs were snoring.

I looked at them. I'd never seen anything but pigs. And they may not have ever seen anything but daisies, but it was all the same as far as they were concerned.

'As for them,' I told my mother, pointing at the gray lumps that were beginning to squeal in the mud, 'they don't even know they're pigs or that they eat daisies, and all that ignorance helps them devour the flowers, which are easy for me to raise.'

My mother disappeared into the house, which she would almost never venture out of, and I gazed at the pigs and at my daisies and inspected the sky, hoping for some sign of rain. If they didn't have the pigs to eat them, the daisies would die uselessly, keeling over on their own stems. Because I don't eat daisies, and my mother doesn't either.